BELLEVUE

A Novel

Marc Siegel

SIMON & SCHUSTER

SIMON & SCHUSTER
Rockefeller Center
1230 Avenue of the Americas
New York, NY 10020

This book is a work of fiction. Names, characters, places, and incidents either are products of the author's imagination or are used fictitiously. Any resemblance to actual events or locales or persons, living or dead, is entirely coincidental.

Designed by Sam Potts
Manufactured in the United States of America
1 3 5 7 9 10 8 6 4 2

Library of Congress
Cataloging-in-Publication Data
Siegel, Marc.
Bellevue : a novel / Marc Siegel.
p. cm.
I. Title.
PS3569.I378B4 1998 97-47546 CIP
813'.54—dc21

ISBN 0-684-83602-5

Acknowledgments

I owe my gratitude to Michael Korda and Chuck Adams for their brilliant editing and to Alice Mayhew for shepherding this book. I would also like to thank my old friend Ken Blaker for his support and help through all the revisions. I am indebted to Jane Howard for her commitment to my work, and to Jack Finkler for his spirit.

To LUDA

PART ONE

IN THE TRENCHES

July 1st

1

*July 1st I became an intern—a blood-*drawing, form-stamping, finger-in-the-rectum machine, an eater of the candy bar dinner. My supervisors were residents—rule-generating, intern-abusing, judges of the great patient write-up, eaters of the candy bar dinner. As an intern, I was an emotional wreck from sleepless nights and growing patient pressures in the era of AIDS, known to the doctors and patients as *the virus*. *The virus* was rampant, afflicting and destroying every organ system known to man until the patient became a constant source of medical need. As an intern, I imagined myself a soldier. The hospital was my trench. I followed the orders of my resident, fighting disease with unthinking zeal. Puddles of *virus* secretion were my land mines. Each *virus* patient had the potential to go psychotic and attack me; each needle I inserted into a *virus* vein had the potential to bounce back and stick me. The whiskey-driven derelict of the 1980s had become the *virus* biter. An intern was the only patrol, protecting the patients from late-night biter assaults. But an intern was also a prisoner. As an intern, I was imprisoned within the unadorned concrete walls of the hospital. The nurses called me day and night for every patient complaint, no matter how trivial. The residents worked me as a slave, using me to generate data for their reports. The patients also considered me their slave, knowing that a complaint to my resident would cause my workload to immediately double. When my resident assigned me an "interesting case," he was shackling me with a disaster—a patient who was constantly on the verge of either dying or going home, but never did either. As an intern, I didn't always know why a patient survived, but when one died, I was usually blamed. Even the administrators abused me. They saved the hospital countless dollars paying me five dollars an hour for hundred-hour work weeks and every fourth night on call. This was such a meager ration of dollars that I told the other members of the on-call skeletal crew we should have become chiropractors.

Bellevue Hospital, lacking any kind of warmth or comfort, was my home. University Hospital, the luxurious arm of the medical center across the river, was my dream. At Bellevue, "continuity of care" was a euphemism for the intern's true plight—continuous care. My patient remained my responsibility even when I wasn't there. Other members of the staff enjoyed "shift mentality." Echoing through Bellevue at two-hour intervals, there was the defiant announcement of the clerks, "Now it's my coffee break . . . Now it's lunch . . . Now it's the afternoon break . . . Now I'm gone."

Two days before internship was due to start, I had received a letter from Dr. William Kell, a senior faculty member, notifying me that I'd been assigned to a special team. I was excited and eager to begin. Apparently my good grades in medical school and my excellent standing with my professors had landed me a privileged position at Bellevue. I could hardly wait to turn this advantage into results; I imagined dispensing the newest medications to cure the most difficult patients.

But when I arrived at the hospital at 7:30 A.M. on Tuesday, July 1st, a half hour before my first rounds, I discovered the sign REMEDIAL TEAM posted on the glass enclosure of my new doctors' station. In a panic, I telephoned Dr. Kell's office. A recording told me that he was out of town on a research project, and that his secretary would be in at ten o'clock.

At 7:45, my new resident, Dr. Goldman, came slouching down the hall. He was smoking a cigarette, and he appeared unable to catch his breath. His clothes looked as if he'd slept in them. He was formlessly obese, a man of prodigious weight. Glaring at me, he taped another sign to the wall glass of the doctors' station—OBSESS OVER THE TEST RESULTS OR YOU'LL OBSESS OVER A DEAD PATIENT.

I reached out my hand, but Goldman didn't shake it.

"I'm a chief resident," he said. "It's bullshit for a chief resident to be assigned to a ward team. The usual role of a chief is to prepare conferences and lectures. I'm supposed to read journal articles," he said angrily, "not baby-sit you."

I knew of Goldman's reputation as a researcher. He was the first resident in Bellevue's long history to have authored an article accepted for publication in the world-renowned *New England Journal of Medicine*. Where had he found the time to study "The Nocturnal Penile Tumescence of Laboratory Chimpanzees as a Function of Their REM Sleep Cycles"? The transition from these heights back to the grueling wards was not likely to be easy for him, even with the best group of interns.

"How come the sign says remedial team?" I said. "I thought this was supposed to be an honors team."

"Honors team, my ass, Dr. Levy. With the crappy medical school you went to?"

The medical school I'd attended in Connecticut had been in danger of losing its accreditation. Though I'd been a top student, apparently Bellevue machismo required the discounting of all medical knowledge acquired at an inferior institution. But if I needed more teaching, why was I being given a resident who was too pissed off to teach me?

And if my schooling was unacceptable, why had they accepted me here in the first place?

Before I could ask Goldman these questions, our medical students arrived: two tall, awkward-looking males, and a shorter, smiling female. It was difficult to believe that these three came from the same classroom. The two males, Michael and Bruce, wore glasses and carried clipboards full of data, apparently reluctant to replace the textbooks of the first two years of medical school with the live patients of the third year. They both wore stiff starched white coats buttoned all the way to the top button. At first glance they looked entirely impersonal and asexual. Delia Meducci, the female student, didn't have a clipboard. She also wore a white coat, but it was open, revealing her low-cut blouse. She was clearly more self-assured and confident than the other two students. She pointed to Goldman's decree, taped to the wall glass. "Obsess over a dead patient," she said, "and it's Goldman's ass."

I looked at Goldman, who smiled and took a long drag on his cigarette.

From the moment the patient chart rack was wheeled from the cramped doctors' station to the open hallway, signaling the beginning of our first rounds, Delia flirted openly. She placed her elbows on the chart rack and leaned forward so that her breasts bounced against the chart rack whenever Goldman removed a patient's chart for our examination. Certainly Delia was good looking, with her dark features and light-green eyes, but it was her provocative posture that first drew everyone's attention.

The other intern on the team, Sal Vertino, finally arrived at five minutes past eight, enduring a vicious glare from Goldman. Sal was dressed in surgical scrubs, a usual intern's outfit, but too casual for the first day. We'd been close friends for years, but as he approached the chart rack, he looked away from me. Recently, I'd become worried for Sal, as he'd taken to staying out all night, rarely eating or sleeping, yet belittling me for my concern.

We'd known each other since early childhood and had attended high school, college, and then medical school together. All through these years, Sal, who came from a family of doctors, had geared me toward this moment when we would finally hit the wards as interns. When we had been accepted to the same residency program at Bellevue, we'd been ecstatic with plans of co-healing and co-diagnosing. We'd envisioned scores of patients bragging to each other that their doctor was Vertino or Levy. These patients would wait for us in their beds, sure that our arrival on rounds signified the beginning of their recovery. But these dreams of fancy cures suddenly seemed ludicrous in the daylight of Goldman's chart rack. If we weren't smart enough at the start to merit Goldman's attention, how could we advance?

On first seeing Sal, Goldman stopped long enough to tell the students that we had been accepted as interns only because Sal's grandfather had trained at Bellevue and still had enough influence to push us past the admissions committee. This notion, true or false, made me feel even more insecure. I silently vowed to be a more sensitive resident when my turn came. If I could never be as successful as

Goldman, at least I would be more concerned with the feelings of my interns.

Goldman and Sal both eyed Delia closely. They seemed absorbed by her body's refusal to obey the usual conventions of space or decorum. The bones of her face were sharply angled. Her green eyes were hard and didn't reveal emotion. We were going to be isolated at Bellevue, kept from normal socializing, confined to our small group. We would spend our time with disease. An attractive woman seemed to be a mirage.

I could immediately sense her need to dominate, to always be the one in control. This made me feel anxious, and I held back from introducing myself. But the first time she had something to say to me, she approached me without introduction and said it right into my face.

"Where do interns sleep here?" she asked. "Where are the on-call rooms?"

Her voice was high pitched, almost electric.

"I don't expect to sleep much," I muttered, and turned away. My answer clearly wasn't what she was expecting. In fact, she seemed surprised that anyone could dismiss her so easily. Delia's striking looks didn't impress me, though I was concerned with how quickly she distracted Sal.

Even with everyone present, Goldman still didn't start rounds right away. Instead, he leaned against the chart rack for several minutes, openly gazing at Delia. But Delia stared at Sal. The contrast between the two men was striking. Sal was trim and muscular; his sleeveless scrub shirt showed off his well-developed tanned biceps. His dark, curly hair was wet, probably from a recent shower, and he wore an expensive musk-scented cologne. By contrast, Goldman was all fat. He was actually known around the hospital as "Fat Goldman." He hadn't shaved. His clothes were creased and stained, and he smelled like one of the unshowered patients.

Fat Goldman, a seamless combination of authority and neurotic shtick, was wrapped together in a three-hundred-pound package. Few doctors still smoked, whereas Goldman chain-smoked unfiltered cigarettes. He had set up the chart rack in the hall directly beneath a NO SMOKING NO FOOD sign, and instead of spewing forth medical wisdom, he nibbled on an old salami, guzzled soda from a two-liter plastic container, stared at Delia, and blew smoke into our faces.

Goldman's authority seemed complete; it was difficult to believe that he answered to an attending physician, a member of the faculty, who possibly was even more overbearing than Goldman. I didn't dare question Goldman's unshowered smell or his filthy clothes, though he immediately questioned my clothes. The Bellevue laundry had dispensed me intern whites that were discolored from a former intern's use—stained brown from antiseptic and red from blood. I wore this uniform proudly the first day, imagining the successful intern (now a resident) who had cured countless patients in these clothes the year before. But Goldman, despite his own disgusting costume, insisted that I return to the laundry after rounds and exchange my used clothes for new issue.

Goldman's hypocrisy characterized him from the outset. He demanded that we be serious and attentive to him, while he joked with every resident who passed the chart rack. Goldman flirted with Delia and ignored the rest of the team. I wondered if he would be of any use to us, even when faced with a serious medical situation.

At 8:15, Dr. Goldman finally began his introductory remarks.

"An intern," he said, "does not save patients. An intern draws blood, puts in intravenous lines, and carries out the orders of the resident. An intern doesn't know enough medicine to be an advocate for the patient. An intern trying to make decisions is a missile without radar guidance."

"How do I learn to be a resident?" Sal asked.

Goldman scowled. "Gradually. Quietly."

"Who teaches you?" Sal said.

"I am the chief resident."

"Who teaches you?" Sal repeated.

Goldman seemed angry, and he started to say something, but a nursing supervisor interrupted him. She was very tall, and she wore an antiquated nurse's cap that held her hair up. She looked to be in her mid-forties and was decisive in a way that came from years of supervising, preceded by years of direct patient care. I suspected she was one of those nurses who had an intuitive feel for a patient's diagnosis long before a doctor finally ordered the right test to prove it. She addressed herself only to Goldman, except for an occasional side glance at the rest of us. It was, as I would come to know, an annual ritual: July 1st, the nurses were full of dread. They braced themselves to endure weeks of indecision, improper orders, and poor communication, as interns learned to medicate, and beginning residents learned to supervise. The nursing supervisor looked with relief to Goldman, because, despite being a slob, he represented a known standard of medical care. He represented the nurses' best hope that things would eventually normalize, that interns under his tutelage could be converted from fumblers to finessers.

The nursing supervisor informed Goldman that one of our new patients had been transferred to the ward from the cardiac care unit the night before. The team we were replacing had forgotten to discontinue lidocaine, a powerful cardiac drug. The nursing supervisor suggested that this drug could cause confusion, and Goldman nodded in agreement. Apparently, the patient was becoming more and more confused. The outgoing team had not been available to advise the nurses the night before, because the outgoing faculty attending had taken them all to a local restaurant for a "Good-bye to Bellevue" dinner.

We followed the nursing supervisor to a room in a remote section of the ward. An obese woman the size of Goldman had ripped off all her monitor wires, and the monitor alarms were sounding. She was standing up in her bed and holding her arms over her head.

"This is your patient," Goldman said to Sal. "I'm assigning her to you. What do you want to do?"

"Watch out! She's going to dive," Delia said abruptly. But Delia didn't move. Sal responded to Delia's shout by rushing over to the bed and tackling the woman just as she was about to dive to the floor.

The nursing supervisor placed the woman in wrist restraints until the effects of the lidocaine could wear off. The supervisor's face, no longer a rigid mask, had loosened into a smile. She proclaimed Sal a hero and shook his hand. Goldman erupted, shouting that Sal Vertino had the worst background of any intern Goldman had ever taught. But the nursing supervisor clearly respected Sal—a doctor who took charge, solving a problem decisively. "How bad could I be?" Sal said. "I've already saved a life."

Now my optimism was renewed. Perhaps Sal and I could develop an alliance with the nurses that would protect us, at least partially, from Goldman's arbitrary decrees. I had learned in medical school that if the nurses approved of you, they could cover for your mistakes and ease your sleepless nights.

Sal Vertino had always been daring. In high school, he was the first to drive a car, the first to have sex with a girl, the first to decide to go away to college. I was more cautious; I rarely tried anything before it was tested by Sal and found to be safe. But Sal didn't care if something was safe. He was after the thrill. He drove his sports car a hundred miles an hour around hairpin turns, rarely resorting to the brake. He never used a condom unless his partner insisted on it. As a teenager, I had alternately scolded Sal and admired him.

How had a suburban town in New Jersey turned out someone so provocative? Sal's lack of parental supervision was unusual for our town. His father had died from the tuberculosis he'd acquired as an intern at Bellevue in 1966. Early medication for tuberculosis had been available but was often misused at Bellevue. Sal's mother had used the money from a life insurance policy to purchase the large corner house two blocks from our house, but then she died of a viral illness affecting her heart while Sal was still in high school. Sal's closest remaining relative was his grandfather, Dr. Giuseppe Vertino, who ran a country medical clinic in Catskill, New York. He allowed Sal to finish high school in New Jersey, unsupervised. Giuseppe had himself acquired tuberculosis during his internship at Bellevue in 1932, becoming one of the last patients to recuperate on the riverboats that were used at the time to quarantine tuberculosis patients. From there he'd moved to Catskill, opening his clinic on the western bank of Hudson's river.

Sal and I were both *A* students in high school, though Sal never studied. His mother, while she was alive, didn't restrict his freedom. She was a sickly woman with wax-colored skin and a compromised posture years before acquiring her fatal illness. In the month before her death, Sal became her around-the-clock caretaker; he said he was respecting her wishes to be kept at home. Afterward, I rarely saw Sal around the neighborhood. In the summer, he worked for his grandfather. In the fall, Sal returned two or three weeks after classes resumed. His Catskill stories were descriptions of big fish caught after a struggle, local shopkeepers' daughters brought willingly deep into the woods, and bleeding patients who stopped bleeding when Sal sewed in the saving stitch.

Sal never got along well with our peers. He cloaked his rage and bitterness in a carefree fuck-it-all attitude. Years later, I finally understood how self-critical he was; the lifelong absence of his father and the sudden loss of his mother left him unsure how to govern himself.

We attended the same Ivy League university. Sal's grades faltered. He was hardly ever in his dorm room or in the library. He dated several different women, though never any one woman for longer than a month. Only one medical school accepted him, a small institution in Connecticut. I decided to go there also, despite the school's marginal reputation, when they agreed to fund my research project on mouse immunity to *the virus*.

In medical school, Sal once again did well without studying. He appeared to have a natural aptitude for every subject, while I prepared for hours for every quiz. My grades were good, but I never completed my research project.

We both selected the combined Bellevue/University program as our first choice for internship. Sal said he admired its reputation for hands-on learning. Our interviewers asked us why we'd decided to become doctors. Sal's reply: because his father had been a doctor; because his grandfather was a doctor; because he'd invested too much time to change his mind. I said, "Because my father was never a doctor."

We were accepted into the program. There were rumors that the hospital had been paid off. I rented a small apartment across the street from Bellevue, and Sal took over the ground floor of a brownstone three blocks away that belonged to a woman he'd been dating, a blond literature professor in her late thirties who was about to leave for a year's sabbatical in Europe.

Back at the chart rack, Goldman assigned us the rest of our patients. Sal's next patient was a suspected biter. Sal accused Goldman of assigning him a biter deliberately, to put Sal at risk of *the virus*. Goldman laughed. "*The virus* is everywhere," he said.

My first patient was Larcombe, the roommate of Sal's biter. Goldman led us down the hall to their room. The Biter was missing from his bed by the door. Larcombe lay absolutely still in his bed by the window. I spoke to him, but he didn't respond. I touched his arm, then shook him, but he still didn't move. His eyes were open, directed at the ceiling. He seemed uncomprehending. This was the only two-bedded room on the ward. Why was this patient without sentience given the best room, with a clear view of the river? According to Goldman, Larcombe's hospital stay extended back past scores of interns and residents, and was punctuated by every medical complication imaginable. How could he ever be discharged from the hospital?

Next to Larcombe's room was the dirty utility room, an intern's potential hangout. It was almost identical to the clean utility room. Each had the same mops and brushes, the intravenous poles, a metal sink, bins for dirty laundry, and countless rolls of tape and gauze. But at the far end of the dirty utility room, there was a small janitor's closet. I imagined an intern and a nurse lying shoulder to shoulder in a carnal alternative to sleep, gripping the old janitor's mop in a shoulder-banging rhythm, while in the next room Larcombe remained oblivious.

Larcombe seemed to be an easy assignment for an intern, but The Biter was bound to be intolerable. I felt angry for Sal. I knew he would fight back against the abuse, which would make a bad situation worse. Goldman might punish him for each assertion he made in his own defense.

I examined Larcombe, listening to his chest with my stethoscope, while Delia and Sal sat together at the end of Larcombe's bed. Did Larcombe have a disease they could catch? Something that was transmissible from nose to nose in water/mucoid droplets? *The virus* was more difficult to acquire.

The Biter returned, limping into the room, leering at us intensely from his bed. He wasn't physically imposing. He had a slight build, a long, hanging jaw, and a pointed chin. He was dressed in a hospital gown that had a dark stain on the front of it.

Goldman observed Sal flirting with Delia on the bed and ordered him to insert the Swan-Ganz into Larcombe. I knew from medical school that the Swan-Ganz was the most invasive, the most complex catheter, invented by Swan and Ganz for use only in the ICU where it was hooked up to the most advanced monitoring equipment. The catheter was supposed to be inserted by an expert physician through a needle into a large vein in the neck.

From there, it was threaded all the way into the heart, and then, with a great deal of finesse, floated around the heart and into the lungs. Its readings on lung pressures were essential to saving the lives of critically ill patients in the ICU.

"The Swan-Ganz?!" Sal protested. "Are you serious? Here?"

"Leave the decisions to me," Goldman grumbled.

"But Larcombe's my patient," I said.

"You assist Vertino."

From the neighboring bed, The Biter offered to assist.

Goldman left us there, actually expecting two clueless interns to insert the Swan-Ganz unsupervised. Delia wanted to stay, but Goldman insisted that she accompany him back to the doctors' station.

Bruce and Michael, the other two medical students, ran to the ICU and returned two minutes later with the Swan-Ganz kit. They watched me fumble with it; their excitement and eagerness at being part of an advanced undertaking so early in the rotation turning quickly to boredom and disappointment when they realized I didn't know what I was doing. Soon they too left the room.

Sal looked at me disdainfully as I tried to assemble the equipment for the procedure. I was furious. I suspected that Goldman was taking us ever further from standard medical practice as he competed with Sal. Rather than the orderly, plodding rounds I'd come to expect from medical school, these rounds were being distorted by absurdly perilous procedures that interns had no right to perform. While other teams were no doubt going slow, learning their patients at the chart rack from dutiful, careful residents, Goldman was punishing us, placing us and our patients at great risk. But what choice did we have? We weren't in a position to make our own decisions. We didn't have the knowledge or the experience to question Goldman. We had to obey him.

I sterilized Larcombe's neck with Betadine, while Sal continued to sit at the end of the bed. I opened the catheter kit, trying not to contaminate its sterile contents. I laid everything out on the bed, using the packaging for a sterile field. The kit contained a long yellow catheter sheathed in clear plastic, along with two extension ports coded in red and blue. I had no idea how to hook up these three lines, assuming I got the needle into the vein and somehow managed to get the yellow catheter through the needle and all the way up into the heart. It was a preposterous task, since a fully assembled and inserted Swan-Ganz was only of use when attached to an ICU monitor. The kit had two different kinds of needles, one impossibly thick and the other long and slender.

"How am I going to insert *both* of these needles?" I said to Sal.

"Only one is for the patient," he said. "We'll use the other one on Goldman."

Wasn't this procedure supposed to require two doctors? As I opened a package of sterile gloves I became more and more nervous and uncertain. I'd never even *seen* one of these things put in, let alone done one myself.

"Sal," I said, talking to myself as much as to him.

"We're not responsible for these decisions, yet we have to carry them out. We can't run the cases ourselves. Goldman is going to continue to dump on us, and the more we fight him, the more he'll do it. If we manage to get one of these patients discharged, another one will replace him, equally as difficult. Goldman grinds out his edicts, and we have to follow them."

I didn't think Sal was listening to me, but all at once he donned sterile gloves and elbowed me out of the way. Then he took hold of the catheter and, without hesitating, thrust the needle under Larcombe's skin. Larcombe still didn't move. Tubes emanated from every orifice. Was he alive? The *pop* was the needle breaking through the plastic of Larcombe's tracheostomy breathing tube. There was a large whoosh of air. Sal's hands shook as he withdrew the needle. The Swan-Ganz looked like a snake curling around a victim's head. We were two panicked interns who were relieved when the hole in the breathing tube didn't end Larcombe's wretched life but created a new path for speech. Suddenly he awoke, bellowing. "My name is Larcombe! I demand to see the patient advocate!"

If Larcombe demanded a new intern, the patient advocate would probably tell him that Bellevue was a public hospital; Larcombe couldn't choose his doctor and I couldn't choose my patient. If Larcombe "circled the drain," as interns and medical students called dying, I, as his intern, would be the one to stay by the bed and administer the futile medications. If Larcombe miraculously recovered; if he were discharged to the street and then returned in another disastrous admission, according to the unofficial bounce-back rule, I would again be his doctor. If Larcombe came to the outpatient clinic, it would be to my clinic. Medical school had scarcely prepared me for what I now envisioned to be the rigid dogma of internship. Only Fat Goldman or death could remove Larcombe from my patient list, or The Biter from Sal Vertino's.

The Biter was laughing, mocking us from his bed. Larcombe seemed stable, so we left him—still without an intravenous line—and returned to the chart rack. When Goldman heard about Larcombe's damaged tube, Sal would be punished, probably with another biter assignment. Sal's obvious interest in Delia was risky. Clearly she had hooked both men; no doubt she would soon begin to twist the hooks.

When Sal and I returned to the chart rack, no one was there. Lists of our patients were taped to the wall glass. Apparently, we were expected to complete rounds by ourselves, while Goldman entertained Delia. Little supervision had quickly deteriorated to no supervision.

By the end of the first wearying afternoon, after having drawn what seemed like a hundred bloods and placed a dozen or more IVs, I returned to the doctors' station. Goldman had been unavailable for the entire day. First he'd gone with Delia to play billiards down on the rehab floor. An hour later she'd left him, meeting Sal for coffee, while

Goldman had paced before the chart rack, refusing to answer the questions Bruce, Michael, and I directed at him. Now Goldman sat in the doctors' station, his face pressed against the glass, steaming it up with his sour breath.

"Dr. Goldman. Can we round on my patients?"

"She cheats," Goldman said. "She pokes me with the pool stick when I shoot."

"When can we go over my patients?"

Goldman growled, seeming to notice me for the first time. "Do your work," he said.

"It's done. Except for Larcombe's IV."

Goldman shrugged. "He doesn't need an IV. He gets everything by feeding tube."

"What about the Swan-Ganz? You told us to put in the Swan-Ganz."

Goldman looked at me as though I were crazy. "No way. You must have misinterpreted me. That catheter is only for the ICU."

"But we tried . . . you ordered us to do it . . . we punctured his breathing tube . . . he's talking now . . ."

Goldman's interest in Larcombe was waning. "Do your work," Goldman said, dismissing me.

He was despicable, questioning me, then ignoring me, ignoring the patients. As a beginning intern, I wasn't sure of many things, but I was certain that he'd ordered us to do the line. Then he'd abandoned us. On my own, I was a gurney with stuck wheels, an ambulance boat without a rudder.

I wasn't scheduled to be on call for several days, another apparent snubbing by Goldman. At 8 P.M., I signed over my patients to the proud intern who was taking call that first night. He was another tall, thin fellow with glasses—Michael and Bruce looked like his clone. In fact, the first thing he said to me was that he'd attended medical school here. Where had I gone? When I told him, he grimaced. He questioned me about my patients—what medications were they on, which tests were in progress, how long were they going to stay in the hospital?—as if I were his intern and he were my resident. My answers didn't seem to satisfy him. I sensed that he was really the same as I was, no smarter, but he was probably on the fast track; perhaps he was being earmarked for chief residency from day one. And he had the benefit of a real resident to teach him all the right steps. His resident was built like a football player. I'd noticed him encouraging his interns with claps on the back as the team huddled before the chart rack.

As the on-call intern was leaving, he admitted that he knew about the problems on our team. "Goldman hates you guys," he said. "He's not about to teach you. He wants you to drop out as fast as possible so he can get on with being chief."

"Why us?" I said. "He just met us. What does he have against us?"

The on-call intern walked off, ignoring my question as if he would be contaminated by hearing too much of my struggle.

"Good luck," he called back when he was almost out of sight.

* * *

Overwhelmed with the events of the first day, I was too anxious to sleep much that night. Toward morning, however, I decided that with all the training still ahead maybe things could improve.

When I came in the next morning, the on-call intern updated me on my patients. I could already see his machismo developing. He had worked all night without a break. Now he was post-call; he walked the stiff-legged post-call walk. His clothes were covered with fresh stains. He seemed to know my patients better than I would ever know them. He'd survived the first night of skeletal staffing, and now he strutted at having been chosen.

The second morning, Sal and Delia didn't show up for rounds and Goldman canceled them. He moped around the chart rack and the doctors' station. I followed him, but he still refused to answer my questions. Sooner or later he would have to give me some direction. In the meantime, what could I do? Who could I turn to? Our attending was out of town. The chief of medicine was as inaccessible as a king. The chief resident, who normally oversaw the resident, was, in this case, also Goldman.

So I rounded on the patients myself. Bruce and Michael were of no assistance because they correctly saw me as having little authority. I compiled my patients' test results, waited for Goldman's direction, and became more and more frustrated.

I was on my way out of the hospital at 9 P.M. when I encountered Sal. He looked pale and fatigued. I wondered if he'd spent the day in the janitor's closet with Delia.

"Fat puts on a white coat," Sal said, proclaiming his independence from Goldman. "He thinks it makes him a great doctor. But he's a mean slob."

"We have to give him a chance. He knows a lot of medicine."

"*Me* give *him* a chance? He's after my Delia."

We shuffled along with our heads lowered. I followed Sal toward the hospital parking lot.

"You've had sex with her, I assume. Tell me what she's like. Where in the hospital do you go? Do you do it in the janitor's closet? Or in the on-call rooms?"

Sal frowned. "No sex yet. This is the longest I've ever had to wait."

"Two days? Sal, Goldman's jeopardizing your career. Let him pursue her."

"Are you interested in her, Levy?"

"Definitely not. She's out of my league."

Sal laughed at me, believing that everyone was interested in Delia. He was wrong, though. Her histrionics unsettled me, even repelled me.

Clearly Sal was obsessing as well as pursuing. He'd researched Delia Meducci's background as completely as Michael and Bruce had researched their patients. As we approached the parking lot, Sal told me what he'd discovered. Apparently, Delia's father was a famous psychiatrist who'd invented and marketed a new line of antidepressants. He admitted his patients to University Hospital, the insured man's alternative to Bellevue, located on the other side of the river. Dr. Meducci was a University trustee as well as a frequent donator of big sums. He owned several houses in different parts of the United States, one of which, according to Sal, was located in Hastings-on-Hudson, New York.

I suspected that Delia's success as a student was her emergence from her father's shadow. According to Sal, she'd turned down admission to her father's alma mater in New Haven in order to attend this medical school, where she was currently at the top of her class. Her fellow students gossiped that her famous father rarely spoke with her, and that he spent most of his time out of town. Delia's mother was known to be a psychiatric inpatient at a plush private facility in Rye, New York. Rumors had spread among the medical students that Delia's father treated her mother cruelly, locking her away in Rye to keep her out of the way of his many love affairs.

How could Sal ignore Delia's twisted family background? She craved male attention, and Sal seemed ready to accept her flirtations as significant. Deprived of a real family, was he so desperate to be loved?

As we reached the entrance to the lot, Sal stopped. "Come on, Levy. Let's take a drive," he said.

"It's too late," I protested. "We have to be back at the hospital early in the morning."

Sal ignored me, heading into the darkness of the lot. I followed him, planning to watch him drive away. But as he revved up the engine of his Alfa convertible, I was suddenly infected with the need to feel the speed, and I opened the passenger door and jumped in. We careened out of the parking lot to First Avenue. At Thirty-fourth Street, we turned right and soon were headed north on the highway, past a trouble spot where during the day a construction crew was repairing a section of guardrail. Cosmetologists of the metal, they brought their trucks and electric hammers, and even when they weren't working, kept us narrowed to one lane with an array of rubber cones.

The highway followed along the river, which was covered with fog, camouflaging University Hospital on the other side. Barges and tugboats passed by unseen; occasionally there was the mournful bass blast of a foghorn.

Once past the construction, Sal increased our speed. We continued on the highway to the Major Deegan Expressway, then to the Saw Mill River Parkway. We exited thirty minutes later at Hastings-on-Hudson, where the side roads were poorly lit and the houses were over a hundred years old.

"Where are we going to sleep tonight?" I asked, as we continued on to smaller and smaller roads, wheels screeching in a neighborhood where large willows and oaks lined the streets. "Have you been here before?"

Sal didn't answer but kept up our speed until we came to an unlit road. He slowed, but didn't stop, driving on past a DEAD END sign to a house that oppressed me from the first time I saw its dark shutters and massive stone facing. He shut off the engine, and we glided by the mailbox and gate up to the driveway, finally coming to a stop behind a black BMW sedan. Without the car noise, I could hear the sounds of water. Unseen, Hudson's river flowed by close behind the house.

The lights were on in the front of the house, but we did not get out of the car. Minutes passed, until the screen door opened and a woman came out onto the porch.

Sal hesitated. "She doesn't see us," he whispered.

"Then why is she out here?"

Her view of us may have been blocked by the BMW, but we could see her. Without the short medical-student coat, Delia seemed taller, curvier. For the tense males of the chart rack, she was their fantasy woman. In the dark surrounding her home, she appeared also to be mysterious.

"Let's go in," I said.

"Wait."

"She knows it's you."

"She doesn't see me."

She turned back toward the door, and I thought she called something into the house.

Sal put in the clutch and we rolled slowly back down the driveway.

"Wait. We're not going to go in? Why did we come here?"

In the street, he started the engine and we sped off, hurtling around a turn, coming up on a white pickup truck that was parked along the curb. Sal didn't brake; he continued to accelerate. At the last possible second, he swung the steering wheel to the left and we veered by. The compressed wind between the two vehicles made a harsh whooshing sound.

"You must be crazy," I shouted at him.

"She wasn't alone."

"That's all the more reason you should stay away from her."

He was silent. My warning was overwhelmed by the noise the car made as he drove on, speeding, skidding up the entrance ramp to the Saw Mill River Parkway, bringing us out of the country, taking us back in the direction of Bellevue.

2

By the third day of internship, I was overwhelmed. Illness was obscured by paperwork. Yesterday's patient was today's death certificate. An empty bed was merely a bed awaiting the next admission.

I rectalized all new admissions, gauging personality by sphincter tone. Some patients refused their rectal, others seemed to welcome it. Still others balked, then relaxed.

The laboratory computer didn't work, so I searched for test results in books. Books in one lab led me to books in other labs. My results always seemed to be buried under pages of other interns' results.

I wrote MD on prescriptions, on charts, on lab slips. I loved writing MD. I wrote it on walls, on candy bar wrappers, on the balcony railings of Bellevue. Where did Fat Goldman write his MD? I wondered.

Fat Goldman was it for me. I awaited his smell, and the look he had when he came waddling up to the chart rack. Just before 8 A.M., I anticipated the arrival of the rumpled Goldman lab coat. His shirts were always open at the collar, and each day he wore the same loosened necktie that was the color of its stains. He smoked his unfiltered cigarettes down to the nub. He sipped bubble gum–colored soda from a two-liter plastic container. This man was supposed to give us counsel.

Sal said our only teachers were the patients.

On the third morning, Michael and Bruce seemed more nervous. They asked Goldman if they could get a cup of coffee, and he said no. They complained of two days of constipation from eating in the hospital cafeteria. Goldman ignored them.

"There are going to be some changes made," he said.

Calling off the names of seven of Vertino's patients, Goldman said they were now assigned to me. He also had a new scheme for the students. Delia would work exclusively with Goldman and the males would work with me. Sal had only three remaining patients and he would work alone.

Goldman took a prescription pad from his lab coat

pocket. He hurriedly wrote out two prescriptions and crumpled them into the hands of Michael and Bruce.

"For laxatives."

Goldman nodded to Delia, and they left the doctors' station abruptly. Michael and Bruce seemed stunned. Once again, there were no rounds, and we were left to treat our patients by ourselves.

Delia appeared to be responding to Goldman's crude displays of authority. Despite his grotesque appearance, she stroked his arm.

Sal was angry. He stood in the hallway and watched them walk away. Sal probably cared more about forfeiting Delia than about forfeiting his patients. Whereas my clipboard listed my patients with a box next to every pending test, Sal's clipboard started with Delia's name and ended with descriptions of women in white nursing uniforms. Over his column of boxes Sal had written Phone Numbers.

He worked the hallway as if it were a singles bar. He thrust out his long, masculine, dimpled chin as if it were a fishing lure. He was outfitted in the same surgical scrub suit and ten-year-old sneakers as the first day, but he hadn't shaved since then. He no longer wore his expensive deodorant. Yet, despite his poor grooming, after just ten minutes he'd attracted an audience of four nurses. He joked with them, his face creasing and lifting when he laughed. The nurses laughed back nervously.

I interrupted, making a big show of needing Sal's help with the patients. Sal took my cue and made an even bigger show of going with me; he was a doctor about to save lives.

The nurses smiled, knowing him as the hero who'd tackled the patient on opening day. I was happy to see his attention diverted from Delia, though I doubted he would replace an obsession for one woman with another.

We went first to Larcombe's room. Today, The Biter was held to his bed with four-point restraints. Unfortunately, mouth gags were outlawed at Bellevue, even in the case of a known biter.

"I ain't touching this guy," Sal said.

"You have to."

"Rule number one, Levy. I don't have to do anything."

"What if he dies?"

"How many has he killed?"

"You're still his doctor."

"Fuck him. He has *the virus.*"

Sal watched as I put on gloves and began to draw The Biter's blood.

"Goldman takes away my patients and leaves me this?"

The Biter struggled to free himself from his restraints. He leaned over the railing of the bed and tried to bite me as I took his blood. Sal reached out his arm and smacked The Biter in the face. He settled back down.

"Son of a bitch," Vertino said, looking at his arm. "The fucker almost got me."

The Biter smiled, his lips separating to reveal his jagged teeth.

"I demand to see the patient advocate," he said coolly.

Sal went to the other bed to check on my patient. Larcombe was once again staring fixedly at the ceiling. On his bedside table, a pocket chess set lay open, its magnetic pieces set in the starting position for a game.

"Is he still alive?" Sal asked.

"Check his pulse."

"Can't feel one."

"Is he warm?"

Sal nodded.

"Then he must be alive."

Larcombe was alive by the numbers. He was fed by feeding tube. Stool and urine were taken from him by catheters. Oxygen was delivered via prongs into his nostrils. He had no known family, no living will, and he was in no condition to sign a do not resuscitate order. But Goldman had said that Larcombe wasn't to be moved to intensive care under any circumstances. He would stay here as long as his skin stayed warm. A plastic body bag was in his closet, awaiting him. I watched his mouth for the O sign, a widening that predicted the end was imminent.

"Goldman wants us to end up like Larcombe," Sal said as we left the room.

In the next room there were three relaxed and smiling patients who belonged to another group of interns, and a fourth, still assigned to Sal, who was having trouble breathing. Her skin was dusky. Sal went to her bedside. She nodded at him. "I'm Sarah Ryan," she gasped.

"You need to draw an arterial blood gas," I said. "And you need to check a chest X ray."

Sal wiped the sweat from the old smoker's face. "Please," she muttered. "Please."

"You need to draw a blood gas."

"I've never done one," he said slowly.

"How? You were an honors student in medical school."

"I was going out with a respiratory therapist, and she drew all my blood gases for me."

I removed the necessary supplies from my lab coat pocket. At Bellevue, the supply bins were mostly empty, and an intern was a walking supply bin, accumulating and hoarding blood tubes, alcohol swabs, needles, and catheters. I swabbed Mrs. Ryan's bluish wrist with alcohol, then stuck her with the blood gas needle. The procedure was painful, but she didn't flinch. I found the artery right away and extracted my sample. Normal arterial blood was bright red, but Mrs. Ryan's blood was much darker.

While I was capping the blood-filled syringe, Sal held Mrs. Ryan's hand. Two nurses came into the room and hooked her up to an aerosolized breathing treatment that neither Sal nor I had ordered. Mrs. Ryan's pallor improved, and she began to breathe easier. Her eyes were closed, and she managed a small smile.

"My son. My son," she said.

The rest of the day was chaotic, although we had neither resident rounds nor attending rounds. Goldman spent most of the day in the hallway, sipping from his two-liter container and talking with Delia. I didn't ask him a single question.

Sal seemed to be avoiding the hallway. Occasionally I would see him in the nurses' station, flirting with whoever was on duty.

The next day, July 4th, was scheduled as a regular workday for us. We were supposed to be on call every fourth night in a four-team rotation. Goldman had scheduled Sal and me to be last, meaning July 4th was our night, but then another wall note indicated he was postponing the rotation by two days, throwing the entire on-call schedule out of whack. I was embarrassed and upset. The intern who was forced to take my place complained bitterly when I told him the news. I offered to make the call up to him on another holiday later in the year, but he looked at me as if he weren't sure I would ever be allowed to take call. I was rapidly becoming an outcast.

Sal didn't come to the doctors' station that morning at all. I pre-rounded for him, drawing his few bloods, checking his test results. The old lunger, Mrs. Ryan, wasn't in her bed, and the nurses said they didn't know where she was.

It was eight o'clock and resident rounds were supposed to be starting, but only Bruce and Michael were at the chart rack. They bragged that they were over their constipation, thanks to Dr. Goldman. They showed me the data they'd been accumulating on my patients. They were working for me like soldiers.

My morning routine was suddenly interrupted when I

heard my name announced by overhead page. "Dr. Levy. Report to the ICU. STAT."

The intensive care unit was a long, narrow room on the south side of the medical floor. This was supposed to be its temporary location until the real ICU was built. Our ICU lacked state-of-the-art equipment. The respirators were the antiquated bellows type with dials and loose turning knobs. There were no multicolored digital monitoring screens or electrical whirring sounds. Portable telemetry monitors were stationed at every bedside. When one of these monitors alarmed, it took a nurse with superacute hearing to tell which bed the sound was coming from. There were rumors of the wrong patient being treated. Sal claimed he'd seen equipment similar to ours in a museum of medical history.

Goldman was standing in the middle of the ICU surrounded by a group of interns and nurses. They were running a cardiac arrest, aka code, on Mrs. Ryan. Her face was even darker than the day before, and she wasn't moving. The pupils of her eyes were dilated. Delia was performing CPR. The interns were watching Delia's breasts bounce as she pumped on the patient's chest.

"Levy!" Goldman barked when he saw me. "Where's Vertino!"

"He's sick."

"My ass, he's sick. Who's looking after his patients?"

"I am."

"Then you're responsible for killing Mrs. Ryan. I hear she's been short of breath since yesterday. Did you tell anyone?"

"I drew a blood gas."

"What a genius. You drew a blood gas. Yesterday! And what about the X ray?"

"It was checked," I lied.

"The patient had lungs that were incompatible with life yesterday! Congratulations, Dr. Levy. It's only the fourth day, and already you've killed a patient!"

Everyone stared. Michael and Bruce quickly left me and stood by Goldman as he took over the chest pumping from Delia. She gazed at him as he groaned and sweated, the fat rolls of his belly undulating like waves of water.

Mrs. Ryan wasn't responding to the code. I was angry. Why should I be blamed when Goldman was supposed to be in charge? The patients were his responsibility. If he wasn't available to guide us, then codes were bound to happen all the time.

"Dr. Goldman," I said, ready to defend myself. But no one seemed to be listening. "Dr. Goldman," I shouted. Still I was ignored.

Sal entered the ICU carrying an X-ray folder.

"Levy!" he whispered. "A night nurse took me out to breakfast."

I couldn't bear to look at him.

"Hey, Vertino's supposed to be sick," either Bruce or Michael said.

"Your lung patient is here," I said. "We're about to pronounce her dead."

"It can't be Mrs. Ryan," Sal said, moving closer to the bed.

Goldman eyed Sal with obvious hatred. He clearly couldn't wait to attack him.

Goldman turned the CPR over to Bruce, who began to pump on the patient's chest as though CPR were a contest of strength. I expected to hear the sound of ribs cracking like chicken bones any moment.

Goldman slowly approached Sal. "Hey, hero," he said. "She's your patient. Did she have a good blood gas when you left yesterday?"

"Yes."

"Bullshit. That blood gas Levy did was the baseline of a corpse."

"I know," Sal said. "I repeated it."

"Sal," I whispered. "You're lying. You've never done a blood gas in your life."

"You must have missed the artery, David. I followed your technique, only the blood I got was bright red and pulsating."

Sal showed Goldman his clipboard. Overnight, Sal's bookie sheet for nurses had been replaced by a list of patients. Next to Ryan's name, Sal had recorded *both* blood gas results.

"Why didn't you tell me this yesterday?" Goldman growled.

"You? You'd already left. I told your covering resident."

"Did you show him the X ray?"

"Of course. It was fine."

Goldman laughed, sensing another opportunity to humiliate Sal.

"You call this fine?"

Goldman took an X ray from a corner of the patient's bed and thrust it at Sal. In response, Sal removed an X ray from the folder he was carrying and thrust it at Goldman. Delia looked from one to the other.

"Look at the names!" Sal said. "Someone mixed them up. Yours isn't Mrs. Ryan. It's Larcombe!"

Goldman studied both X rays, and his expression changed. He retreated to a corner of the ICU and twisted open a new two-liter bottle of soda. Delia grinned at Sal, and Michael sidled up to him, eager suddenly to be his student, despite Goldman's orders. Around the ICU, interns shook their fists, accepting Sal into their ranks.

I grabbed my friend by the arm. "Goldman has it in for you," I whispered. "He'll find a way to twist this. Let him have her."

"No way," Sal said, pulling his arm away.

"Think of your patient. You can't bring her back. No matter what you did for her yesterday, Goldman will find a way to make this your fault."

"She crumped suddenly! I had nothing to do with this! She was fine yesterday."

"But he'll hold you accountable for today."

By some miracle, Mrs. Ryan didn't die. She was resuscitated, remaining in the ICU on the creakiest, whirriest, most dysfunctional of all the respirators. The breathing tube molded her mouth into a perfect O sign. She circled the drain, but then, unaccountably, she began to stabilize.

Goldman said that if Mrs. Ryan ever made it back out to the wards, she would be assigned a new set of interns. He continued to blame Sal and me for her condition. He took Larcombe away from me and reassigned him to Sal as a punishment for Mrs. Ryan.

July 5th, Saturday, Vertino came to the hospital earlier than I did. By the time I started my pre-rounds, his were already finished. He drew The Biter's blood without incident. He managed to get a new IV into Larcombe. He worked steadily as if his three patients were ten patients. He passed the nurses in the hallway without responding to their looks. But just when I was starting to recapture the old fantasy of duo cures, Sal spotted Delia in the hallway and went off with her.

At 8 A.M., Goldman stood at the chart rack looking serious about conducting real rounds. I tried to cover for Sal, saying that his car had broken down. I presented data on Larcombe, The Biter, and the obese woman, who no longer tried to dive from her bed. Then I presented data on my own patients, while Bruce and Michael fidgeted. Sensing Goldman's lack of interest, their clipboards were no longer up to date. And Goldman didn't bother to ask them questions. He took long gulps from his two-liter container. He scratched his belly and yawned.

Delia and Sal came up to the chart rack holding hands.

Goldman's voice was an angry croak. "Vertino. The nurses report you left needles in Larcombe's bed this morning."

"So what," Delia said. "The guy never moves. He had a stroke or something. He's dead. Nothing Sal does to him matters."

"That's why he's perfect for Sal," Goldman said.

"No," Delia said, "he's the worst kind of patient for Sal. If Sal helps him, you can deny it. But if he dies, you'll blame Sal for it."

"When did you become the intern?" Goldman said. "Larcombe has hundreds of diagnoses. Sal's supposed to know every one. Has he bothered to read the chart?"

"Why should he?" asked Delia.

"Because that's his job. Is Levy going to see every patient, while Vertino screws around?"

"This is still only the first week," I said.

"Lives are at stake," Goldman said. "Remember Mrs. Ryan?"

"Sal really cares about Mrs. Ryan," Delia said. "And he took good care of her. You just want to punish him."

Despite his authority, Goldman was losing his battle for Delia. Clearly he would punish all of us for this, especially Sal.

"As of right now, Vertino is on probation," Goldman said. "He has zero patients."

Sal shrugged. He seemed more interested in the passion Delia showed in defending him than in his own peril.

"This isn't fair," I said. "Sal comes to work in the morning before I do."

"My ass he does. You know, you two are the worst interns I've ever seen. Levy, you're only acceptable by comparison to Vertino. I wish to hell I'd interviewed you myself and kept you out of the program."

"You did interview us," I said. "Don't you remember?"

"You promised to make us great doctors," Sal said.

Goldman rolled his eyes and flopped his arms down. He came around the chart rack. He approached me so aggressively, I was frightened he might bludgeon me with the bottle he was carrying. Why was he suddenly interested in me, when he'd been ignoring me for days? He grabbed me by the arm and maneuvered me down the hall. The others remained behind. Delia and Sal seemed glad that Goldman was leaving. Michael and Bruce looked bewildered.

"We're going to see the living textbook," Goldman said to me.

The dayroom between the wards was empty with the exception of one patient and one doctor. The patient sat in a bright-green wheelchair. The doctor wore a gray suit and hovered over him. Red spectacles that were intended for a much smaller face squeezed the very tip of the doctor's nose. I was outraged to see that the name on his ID badge was William Kell. Apparently he had returned to town without even bothering to notify us. Whatever his business was with this patient, it was taking the place of the formal attending rounds he was supposed to be conducting with our group. I immediately disliked him.

At the same time, I immediately liked the patient because he was thrusting his artificial leg at Dr. Kell. Instead of a hospital gown, the patient was dressed in a tarnished European suit. Over it he wore a thick coat of what appeared to be rodent fur. His face was filthy, and he exuded a street stench. A greasy beret slanted down over his forehead. An out-of-date prosthesis was held to his hip with a worn leather strap. As soon as he saw me he began to complain. First it was phantom limb pain. Then it was the pain in his real leg. He complained that his bones ground in their sockets. He gestured for me to come closer, and when I did, he pointed at Dr. Kell with a gnarly finger that had a large boil on its middle knuckle.

"We derive our authority from God and the Company and not from a few ignorant physicians."

"Meet Mr. Victor Rulo," Goldman said.

"He thinks he's Peter Stuyvesant," Kell said.

The patient rolled his wheelchair even closer to me. I was practically overcome by the pungency of his odor.

"Consider my disquieting situation," he said. "I am enveloped in a glacial frost. A delegation comes to me at ungodly hours, long before noon, and they insist I consume little white pills. I am tortured, poked, manipulated against my will, and when I protest against their injustice, they tether me to my wheelchair. I was in six Lithuanian prisons where I was treated more mercifully. I ask you, in all sincerity, can a man be expected to live like this? A patient must be given the opportunity to heal. Don't you know that?"

Dr. Kell took notes in a red notebook.

Rulo said, "All I ask is a meal and a view of the river. What is a patient without a bed and a tranquil view?"

"Assign him an intern," Kell said to Goldman.

"A medical intern? Or psychiatric?"

"I don't care. Just someone to keep an eye on him."

"Dr. Levy will do it," Goldman said, and Kell smiled at me.

"I need a room," Rulo protested, "not a useless trainee."

Kell said, "You'll get what I decide to give you."

"I must room with Mr. Larcombe. I must protect him from that ghastly murderer. Oh, the classic American style. The insidious threat."

"You'll protect no one," Kell said.

"But sir, I can be your ally. I can prevent illicit fornications in Mr. Larcombe's bed. Intern copulates with student. Imagine the contamination, to say nothing of the violation of basic aesthetics."

Goldman winced. Could Rulo know about the competition over Delia? Or did he have a psych patient's intuitive aim for sensitive issues?

Goldman left us, retreating down the hall. Kell closed his notebook and followed him. Light reflected off the moving plastic of Goldman's soda container. The gray suit followed the discolored lab coat. "A room, a room," Rulo called after them.

I was being left behind with my new assignment—the most provocative of patients—without a room to contain him.

Kell paused.

"Kell will kill me. Kell will murder me," Rulo shrieked.

"Order up a shot," Kell said. "Get some restraints."

"Me?"

"Do it," he said.

"Do it! Do it! Do it!" said Rulo.

"I'll be right back," Kell said.

I was so nervous, I put my hand inside my lab coat pocket and broke the rubber top off my reflex hammer. Now I would have to use my stethoscope to bang knees. I squeezed my candy bar until the goo ran. Kell and Goldman reached the other end of the hall as Rulo again motioned for me to come closer, which I declined to do.

Though I waited in the dayroom for several minutes, Dr. Kell didn't return. Mr. Rulo wheeled himself to the large glass doors at the center of the dayroom. Opening the doors, he continued out onto a balcony.

Most of the patients' rooms had balconies, but the balcony off the dayroom was the largest. I was curious to see the view. And despite Rulo's exotic words and his disgusting habitus, I found myself compelled to follow him. As I passed through the glass doors, I noticed a dented brass plaque fastened to the balcony railing. The plaque was covered with graffiti. The inscription was rusty and faded and difficult to make out:

> In 1623, Dutch settlers named this land jutting into the river the Fallen Altar, and built an almshouse on the site. Forty years later, British conquerors

recognized the military value of the unobstructed view and renamed the jut of land Belle Vue.

The Union army used the almshouse to shelter wounded troops during the Civil War.

In 1865, Bellevue Hospital was opened.

In 1875, a slaughterhouse and an ashhouse were built across the river. A hundred years later, the slaughterhouse was demolished, and University Hospital was built.

Outside, the morning air cooled me, but Rulo was diaphoretic. I counted his breaths, an intern's reflex. Thirty times a minute his chest lurched, a mournful wheeze. He slumped forward in his wheelchair as I removed his medical chart from a leather pocket in the back. It was the thickest chart I'd ever seen.

I turned first to the medical notes section. Over many months of recording progress notes, Bellevue's doctors had given Rulo twenty major medical diagnoses, though he still lacked the life-breaking one known as the dreaded "rule out;" the one diagnosis such as cancer or *the virus* that removed a patient from the category of health and placed him in the group that awaited a tragic outcome. Patients took their rule out with them everywhere; they couldn't shake it with a pill or an operation. A doctor wanted to rule it out, but sometimes he couldn't.

The social work section of Rulo's chart confirmed what

I'd already guessed—that Rulo roamed the hospital. The staff never knew where they might encounter him. Security didn't restrict him, despite his odd appearance. Social work concluded that assigning him a room was fruitless, since he would never stay in it. There was no outside residence to send him home to, and he continually refused placement in a nursing home.

I looked at Rulo again. He was a small man with a large face. His nose was long and crooked. When he suddenly blew his nose into an old handkerchief, it sounded to me like a shofar blowing in a synagogue on the High Holy Days. His sclera seemed enormous, and his eyes enlarged as he rolled toward me, tiny dark pupils dancing back and forth with nystagmus on a bed of white. His hands were small like ears, but his ears were large and fleshy and looked like the hands of a workman.

As he approached me, the rate of his breathing continued to increase. He tried to trip me with his artificial leg, but I managed to elude him. I leaned against the railing at the edge of the balcony and looked out over the river. All at once, Rulo stopped pursuing me, and he began to talk.

According to Rulo, the modern version of Bellevue was constructed on landfill. The river wasn't a true river but a saltwater tributary off the bay. The midstream land masses were smaller than real islands. Rulo said that during the day, the river borrowed its colors from the land. At night, or on cloudy days, the river reflected the sky. As I stood (and Rulo sat) on the dayroom balcony, thin clouds crossed in front of the sun, and the river turned gray, much the same color as the highway that ran alongside it. As it passed the hospital, the highway rose onto stanchions and curved east onto the landfill. Where the landfill ended, three hundred yards farther north, the highway curved west, descending on smaller and smaller stanchions until it was again level with the river. At this point the highway narrowed and forfeited its shoulder. From the landfill to the narrow stretch, a driver had an unobstructed view of the river for almost a mile. Light reflected off the glass walls of University Hospital on the other side of the river. This was a high-risk section of road, but there were no warning signs.

The police were gathered at the westward curve, and they had closed the southbound lanes to traffic. Police cars were circled like covered wagons. A car had ruptured the metal of the guardrail, and the police were mining the wreck for bodies.

"Vultures," Rulo suddenly shouted at the police. "Carrion pickers." The "miners" continued working. One of them had donned a fireproof suit, and he ignited a blowtorch.

"Headless vultures!" Rulo taunted. "Circle, circle, circle!"

Rulo seemed to think they were pointing at us.

"They want to see your hospital badge," he said. "Show it!"

"They can't see us from down there."

Rulo looked at me as if I were crazy.

The man with the blowtorch had scorched a path into the dead car, and now some of the police were sawing. Others were pulling, trying to bring an object through a space that seemed too small. They pulled it out one part at a time, but all at once it slipped out on its own and collected back into a lump.

"Monsters," Rulo called. "Killers."

The police worked; pulling, collecting. They brought another body into the clear, to where I could see it. I waited for it to move. I watched the chest for its first sharp breath.

And I remembered my medical school. In my first year, I was already the surgeon; the patient was the cadaver of my anatomy class. She was the smallest, less than five feet in length. In life, she would have been called petite. I worked over her cold flesh, wishing I could give her the warmth of my life. I split her open. I knew I was expected to accept her as an object. I wasn't given time for fainting or crying. There was no transition. I hugged and argued and flirted with the other medical students; we all acted as lively as we could. We named our cadavers; mine was Beatrice. Beatrice was the first of many shocks I suffered through as a medical student. In my third year, a real surgeon taught me to cut; I made the first incision into a woman's swollen belly, then I stood by helplessly while the surgeon uncovered a cocoon that became a baby with a startled scream. By the time of my graduation, I had begun to develop a doctor's emotional retreat from which many never returned.

The police were taking more bodies out now, one by one. There was one body that seemed stiffer than the others. It moved like bone moved, coming straight out, the way teeth did.

Rulo rocked back and forth in his wheelchair. The car wreck seemed to have a special meaning to him. "Mourn the fate of the overwrought," he said.

"Horses were safer," I said, and Rulo immediately began to describe the horse-drawn ambulance ride to the old Bellevue Hospital, whose balconies were right on the river. He recounted the early days of the century, when quarantine boats rocked in the shallow water near the shore. Below deck, tuberculosis was treated with cold air and salt spray. The patients cooled until winter came, when either the bacillus died or the patients froze. According to Rulo, upstate sanatoriums took the place of these boats, until, in 1933, the last boat was removed.

The following year the highway was built on landfill. The modern Bellevue Hospital was completed a few years later.

"I can see the quarantine boats," Rulo said. "The steam of their engines reaches me through time."

"No. You can't possibly."

"The cries come to me from the boats. The howls of the sick overtake me as whispers. I can hear them," he insisted.

"No, Mr. Rulo. Not even in your memory. You are only fifty-three."

Rulo looked at me harshly. "Oh, the old balconies," he said, "the rust, heavy with time. Listen for the peoples' pain. Feel the balconies that held lives in their concrete grip."

"No, Mr. Rulo," I said.

"You must consider history," he said.

"Are you saying that *you* were here at the beginning of the century?"

Rulo looked at me again.

"Of course not," he said.

But he did claim that he was descended from Stuyvesant as well as from Henry Hudson. According to Rulo, Hudson had entered the harbor in 1609 with the stealth of a virus entering a cell. As relentless as a Rulo, he had followed a true river as far as its origin, a dead end north of Albany.

It was time for me to go back inside the hospital. Rulo was hard to dismiss, but I had to live at today's Bellevue. Even as I left him, Rulo continued to weave his tale, a dizzying story of his life intermingling with the lives of our most accomplished citizens throughout three hundred years of American history.

I hadn't seen Sal all day. Night was coming on. I signed out to the on-call intern and prepared to go home. On my way out, I finally found Sal in the dayroom, inhaling the sewer smell that still remained there long after Rulo had left.

"Delia and I, we've made love."

"Sal. You're supposed to be working."

"I have no patients."

"Work with me or Goldman might fire you."

"Fuck Goldman."

I looked out through the grease-streaked dayroom window. I could see a line of occupied stretchers between the highway and the river. These men and women were *the bedless,* those who refused hospital admission. Rulo was once a member of this group. They wanted only a gurney and an occasional sandwich to eat. The more charitable of the staff left gurneys outside. Others, less charitable, removed them.

Twenty yards from *the bedless,* Fat Goldman stood under a streetlamp.

"What was it like?" I asked Sal.

"Awesome. She goes and goes. Like a machine."

A black BMW came slowly down the street, stopping beside Goldman. He opened the passenger-side door.

"Oh, shit!" Sal said, seeing what I saw. "How can this be?"

I was stunned too. This went beyond flirtation. Delia was going from having sex with Sal to driving off with Goldman.

Sal ran down the hall. I ran after him, catching up just before Larcombe's room. Larcombe's vacant face was now turned toward us. On the chessboard, the white king's pawn had been moved two spaces forward. As Sal and I ran past, The Biter reached across his bed and moved one of the black pieces.

"Where are we going?" I shouted at Sal, who ignored me.

We reached the stairwell just as Kell appeared at the end of the hall. He motioned for us to stop. But Sal opened the stairwell door, and we vaulted down the stairs.

* * *

We took the Major Deegan Expressway to Route 87. When we were well past the exit for the Saw Mill River Parkway, and I knew we weren't following Delia, the motion of the car calmed me down. We drove until it was night. At ninety miles per hour, the white line pulsed by like electricity. The recurring lights on the side of the thruway were Howard Johnsons, Mobils, and Shells.

"Tell me where we're going."

My only answer was the car moving on the road. Why was I going along? I had to protect him if I could. I had to help him stay at Bellevue. What alternative did he have? The system had formed us. We were what it had made us. In the next rotation, a resident might like Sal for the same passion that made Goldman hate him. In the meantime, Sal had to be patient. Bellevue itself never really changed. Sal could get used to it. Every night, stains grew on the lab coat of a proud on-call intern. Every morning, patients protested against families that had abandoned them. A patient's pain, distilled to a shriek, was finally answered by death.

After another hour, Sal turned on to an exit ramp. He drove us deeper into the woods on side roads he seemed to know would lead us to smaller side roads. Above us, tall trees obscured the moon. The Alfa skidded on dry pavement, barely eluding the bottoms of these trees. We roared on through stop signs, pausing for fractions of seconds at red traffic lights. Occasionally a house went by in a flash of yellow light. The faster and farther we went, the more I felt like an AWOL intern. I white-knuckled the armrest until, finally, we slowed at the WELCOME sign for Catskill. I felt relief. At least now I knew where we were going.

I could hardly hear my voice over the roar in my ears.

"Maybe Giuseppe can help you forget her," I said.

"Not a chance," he replied.

PART TWO

CATSKILL

July 5th

3

Past the Catskill sign, the road became Main Street. A traffic light changed slowly from yellow to red in the intersection ahead of us. Sal floored the gas pedal, and the ten-year-old Alfa Romeo hesitated, then took off. Wind whistled in through a hole in the ragtop. A large truck blared its electric horn. We sped through the intersection, then veered down a dark side road. Without warning, Sal stamped on the brake pedal and the car screeched to a skidding stop. He turned to me in the dark, breathing hard. His eyes seemed unfocused. I thought, *He's going mad.*

"Maybe you're right, Levy. Maybe Pops will have the answer."

"About Delia?"

"About why I've failed. Why I've had to come back here."

"You can't stay here. You have to return to Bellevue."

He didn't answer me. He stared out the window of the car. There was no moon now, and the sky looked like it was about to rain. Off to the side of the road, a field of weeds was blown about by the wind. Sal began to tremble. More and more, he seemed to be losing control of himself. I'd never seen him look like this. I knew we were lucky to have made it safely from Bellevue all the way to Catskill with Sal driving. Leaving the city, I'd been anxious, but the monotony of the highway had calmed me. Now I was almost frantic with apprehension; I would stay that way until I could discuss Sal with Giuseppe Vertino.

But Sal turned off the car engine. For several minutes, he sat listening to the overwhelming silence of the country night, interrupted only by crickets. I knew if I urged him to drive on he would ignore me. When he finally began to speak, his voice was suprisingly calm and measured, and he had stopped trembling.

"Ten miles up this road, there's a stretch of loose gravel. The day I began working at the clinic last summer, a local guy lost control of his truck and skidded it into a ditch up there. He slammed his head against the windshield. The cops brought the body to us. I watched it for hours, and it didn't go cold. Pops called it a 'voodoo death.'"

"Who was he?"

"Worked in the gas station. Shacked up with the town witch. Word was he tried to break it off with her."

"You think she cast a spell?"

Sal laughed horribly. "I know she cast a spell. This was no anatomy-class cadaver. The skin stayed warm, but there was no breathing, no heart beating. I lifted the eyelids, and the eyes were staring at me worse than Larcombe."

"But Larcombe's alive."

Sal glared at me as though I hadn't understood him. "Anyway, Pops went to bed. I got the body ready for the morgue. After I was done, I went out on the porch. I sat there until almost 4 A.M. I heard a dog barking, strange for so late at night. The wind came up, and leaves were flying everywhere. The dog ran past. It was a black beast, I remember the way it turned its head back and snapped its teeth at the air. Levy, the dog acted as if some flying thing were following it. The door of the clinic flapped open and closed in the wind. I said, 'Who is it? Who's out there?' And suddenly there was someone with me on the porch."

"The witch."

He nodded. "She said, 'I knew that driver.' "

"What did you say?"

"Levy, I couldn't move. All I could do was stare at her. She moved closer until she was right on top of me. Her eyes were black darts. 'Why are you here?' she asked. 'It's the middle of the night.' I knew I was trapped. I had to find a way to overcome her. Luckily, at that exact moment I saw the light just starting in the corner of the sky. I pointed to it.

'No,' I said. 'You're wrong. It's not the night. It's the morning.' "

Sal lowered his shoulders, visibly relieved as he recalled the outcome. He stroked the thin stubble that barely covered his chin. "Just then, a phone inside the clinic started to ring. Pops got up to answer it. The next thing I knew, the woman was gone."

"You won," I said.

Sal started the car. "Ever since then," he said, "I've felt that this town is the one place that is safe for me." Sal drove on, accelerating. Over our heads, the wind blew the tree branches in wide circles. But the whine of the car engine seemed louder than the sound of the wind.

"Why was a phone ringing?" I shouted. "Are you saying the spell was broken?"

He smiled, refusing me the satisfaction of an answer. He followed the twisting road. We went deeper in among the trees until we came to an old wooden sign and an opening for Giuseppe's clinic.

According to his grandson, Giuseppe Vertino was known in Catskill for his generosity. He kept a liberal supply of morphine to counter terminal pain, and he never charged his patients more money than they could afford. Sal told me about an old bowl made of polished silver that occupied a place on the front counter of the clinic. Patients could leave cash there if they had any. Sal said the bowl was usually empty, except when the doc himself put money in it for a sick patient who couldn't otherwise afford admission to the local hospital.

According to Sal, his grandfather preferred a ten-gallon hat and boots to the silk and leather clothes he'd brought to America from Italy. He owned a stock of well-oiled rifles and was proud of the few times he'd shot people who were trying to rob him, his only regret being that he'd never actually killed any of them.

Still, Giuseppe was known more for his doctoring than his gunslinging. Early in his career, he was said to have mailed a skin sample labeled "North American blastomycosis" to the state laboratory in Albany. This produced a round of professional laughter, until a pathologist happened to look at the sample under a microscope. There he found the characteristic rings of blastomycosis, a disease that had only seen five documented cases up to that time.

I opened the screen door. The inside door had been removed from its hinges and lay on the ground.

Inside, two large fans stood on the front desk, turned off despite the hot night. Mosquitoes landed on the blades but stayed only for seconds, as if they expected the slicing motion to return. The front desk was also the nurses' station. The silver bowl, an antique engraved with scenes from along Hudson's river, was empty. Bedpans and gynecological equipment were stacked alongside the sink. Pill bottles in perfect rows lined the shelves. Sterile gauze and bandages lay in discrete piles across the counter. A nurse's uniform, bleached a radiant white, hung on the coatrack. Darkness presided here. I could barely make out the two typewriters on the right and left sides of the desk where a more modern clinic would have had computer terminals.

A long hallway went to the back. The walls and floor were hardwood, probably oak. Two examining rooms faced off on opposite sides. Each contained a hand-cranked leather examining table and an overhead examining light, the kind that was once standard in operating rooms. The equipment was old-fashioned, but, from what I could see, the techniques of sterilization seemed modern. I could imagine the young victim of the car accident in one of these rooms, his body glowing with unnatural heat, lacking the rigidity of death, yet awaiting Giuseppe's final pronouncement.

As Sal and I felt our way along the hallway, my eyes became more accustomed to the darkness, and I saw a light coming from the room at the rear of the clinic.

Giuseppe Vertino was in his office. He sat with his feet on the desk, smoking his pipe. He didn't wear cowboy boots or a cowboy hat, just an ordinary pair of jeans and a gray cotton button-down shirt. For the longest time, he didn't say anything. His face was lit by a single lamp. He didn't show surprise at seeing us. The last time I'd seen him was at a holiday gathering at Sal's mother's house several years before. He looked almost the same now as then, perhaps more grizzled. Sal and I stood before him, watching the smoke from his pipe curl upward in perfect circles. Something about his presence inspired me to immediate reverence. What had I expected? A gunfighting scientist? The shrunken chest of an old tubercular? An out-of-date country practitioner? Instead, I sensed his great professionalism. Sal may have exaggerated some of the details, but the main feature was right; this was a man who gave everything he had to his patients, a physician in the way that some men are lovers.

On one wall there was a photograph of two men fishing by a river. One looked to be a younger version of Giuseppe, the other an older version of Sal. On the opposite wall there was a photograph of doctors. They wore high-collared hospital uniforms. The notation was BELLEVUE INTERNS 1932. I couldn't find Giuseppe among the group, probably because of his tuberculosis.

When Sal spoke, his voice was uneven and cracking like the voice of an adolescent. "There's so much pressure, Pops," he said. "I'm afraid of what's going to happen to me."

Giuseppe motioned us to overstuffed leather chairs that reminded me of the clinic's examining tables. In the shadows that crossed the desk, Giuseppe's face looked leathery. His eyes were unexpressive except when they moved, and then they flashed with emotion.

"What do you want me to do?" Giuseppe's voice was soft.

"Let me come here and work with you."

Giuseppe stared at his grandson. "No," he said.

"But, Pops, I'm being set up to fail. Ask Levy. My resident despises me. He competes for my girlfriend."

Giuseppe didn't look at me.

"Vertinos always have women," he said. "So what. I want to know why you aren't working. You must learn to preside over illness."

Sal didn't tell his grandfather that his patients were being taken away.

"Please, Pops," Sal begged. "I have to work here."

"Medicine is your religion. And Bellevue is your house of worship. There is nowhere else for you. At Bellevue the patient trusts you. You cannot fail him. You are not a technician. You are not a genius or an academician. At Bellevue you treat the sickest of the sick, and you cure him; even as an intern, you get him back out to the street. Under your care the street people live practically forever. And wherever you go, to a private hospital or to a country clinic, you take your deep, suffering love for what you do with you. You take it with you. You are proud of who you are. A physician who trained at Bellevue."

Sal lowered his head.

Giuseppe stood. "It's getting late."

"Tomorrow's Sunday," Sal said.

"It's our first day on call," I said, and Sal glared at me.

"Take Dr. Levy back to work."

"Levy can take my car. I won't be needing it here."

Giuseppe put his arm on his grandson's shoulder.

"My internship gave me tuberculosis. They wanted to retire me permanently right then. They stuck me out on the river sanatorium. But I treated the other quarantine patients and it counted toward my internship requirements. The next year I made it back to the wards as a resident."

"Things are different now," Sal said.

"No. Not so different. Promise me you'll fight for your career. I know the kind of student you were, Sal. You can be an excellent doctor."

Sal didn't seem to be expecting his grandfather's praise. For a moment, he brightened.

"Promise you'll give it another try."

"But, Pops. . ."

"Promise me."

Sal hesitated, and I saw the great effect his grandfather, and only his grandfather, had on him.

"Okay, Pops," Sal said finally. "One more try."

Giuseppe's facial muscles relaxed, and he offered to take us to his trout-fishing stream. "The brookies are biting like mad tonight," he said.

"Next time," Sal said, heading down the hall to the front of the clinic.

Sal's emotions were erratic. He was buoyed up by his grandfather, but as soon as we left the clinic and started on our way back, he once again seemed hopeless.

"I'm not going to make it."

"Just promise you'll stop seeing Delia. And things will get better."

He looked at me, twisting his eyebrows until I was sure he was mocking me.

"I'm not going to promise that," he said.

4

*At 8 A.M. Sunday, our first on-call be*gan. When I reached our doctors' station, I found the interns from the other services lined up waiting to sign over their patients to me. Each intern had a large list of patients with complex medical problems that were well beyond my current scope of unsupervised understanding. One after another, the interns signed out, nonchalantly encapsulating their patients in terse medical terms, sandpapering living things into seeming smoothness with the Latinate words of our profession. At first, I was glad that it was Sunday. It was the one day I could pretend that my group was the same as any other group, since *no* group held resident rounds on Sunday. But the departing interns laughed at this idea. Sunday was widely considered the worst day to be on call; if you weren't on call, you got to go home at 8 A.M. It was clear that Sal and I had been saddled with this chore as yet another punishment.

I was informed that Goldman had come in early in the morning and instructed the other interns to sign out only to me, not to Sal.

"Where's Goldman now?" I asked angrily.

No one knew. One of the interns said he was down in the emergency room working up a new admission. Another said Goldman was sleeping in the on-call rooms. A third suggested he had left the hospital with Delia Meducci.

"But the medical students are supposed to be off Sunday," I protested, instigating another chorus of knowing laughter.

Sal arrived after the other interns had left. He was dressed in a fresh shirt and tie and a pair of regulation intern pants. His hair was combed. He'd shaved. He seemed eager to resume his responsibilities. I didn't have the courage to tell him about Goldman's instructions. But Sal must have realized what was happening, since no one was waiting to sign out to him and no one had posted a list of patients for him to cover. He sat in a corner of the doctors' station looking uncomfortable as I went over my list. His hands were clenched, and he ignored several nurses who tried to get his attention as they passed the doctors' station.

At 8:15 one of these nurses alerted me that Rulo's intravenous line had clogged.

"How can Rulo have an intravenous line?" I said. "He doesn't even have a room."

Sal and I located Rulo back in the dayroom. Dr. Kell stood over him with a syringe, injecting a mysterious red liquid into the bag of intravenous fluid that hung on a pole attached to Rulo's wheelchair. Today, Kell was wearing the long white lab coat of a University attending. After a week of internship, we still hadn't had a single attending rounds. How did Kell plan to evaluate us? What was his justification for not teaching us?

"Dr. Kell. Why are you here on Sunday?" Sal demanded. "What are you doing to this patient?"

"Good morning, Dr. Levy," Dr. Kell said, ignoring Sal. "Your patient Mr. Rulo has agreed to be the initial member in my new study."

"Liar!" Rulo roared. "Torturer!"

"What are you studying?" I asked.

"It's a joint venture between the departments of medicine and psychiatry. More than that I can't say."

"Drug-company sponsored?" Sal asked.

Kell continued to ignore him.

"Exploitation," Rulo said. "Guinea pigs for a buck."

"What happened to you last night?" Kell said, opening his red notebook. The intravenous fluid was turning red from Kell's injection.

"Last night!" said Rulo. "Yes. I almost had a bed. I would have had a room, had you not intervened. The intern covering for Dr. Levy detected a fracture, prompting a visit from the master builders. They intended to remove me to the bone floor for further testing, had you not countermanded the order on behalf of this foul, pointless study. On the bone floor, I might have been assigned a working telephone! Imagine, Victor Rulo, safe inside the thickest womb of concrete poured out by these bone men, in a permanent cast."

"Are you saying the orthopedists built their own floor?"

"Of course not. I tell you, I was lying here awake without benefit of a single sleeping pill when the master builders arrived. Tell me, why has my nightly sleeping pill been routinely and cruelly withheld? The nurses ignore me because I haven't a room. They pretend I'm a visitor."

"Why can't you study him on ortho?" I asked Kell.

"They won't take him," he said impatiently. "He doesn't have a fracture. Your coverage was mistaken."

"A gurney arrived. Glad hands carried me onto it. I was whisked through the hallway, only to be returned, by your order, back here to Purgatory, where I lack any sort of proper attention. I seek out the nightly caretakers. I discover a back-room orgy of food and drink—glutted, slovenly caretakers sipping at their soups, drinking dark liquid from oversized mugs."

"The nurses assure me he never left the dayroom," Dr. Kell said.

"Liar!" Rulo said.

"The nurses assure me that you're victimizing this patient," Sal said. "They say you haven't obtained a proper consent for your study."

"That's right," Rulo agreed. "No consent."

Kell glared at Sal. "You'd better worry about your own situation instead of questioning me."

"Are you threatening me?" Sal said.

"Not at all."

"Then why don't you assign me some patients?"

"Prove yourself worthy and I'll be happy to assign them to you."

"How am I supposed to prove myself without patients?"

Kell didn't answer. Sal had pointed out the core hypocrisy. I suspected that Kell enjoyed keeping Sal without options.

"This man is your true enemy!" Rulo said. "You think it's the corpulent one, but this one is your master. He lurks in the background, waiting until your will is spent."

"What about the psych service?" I said to Kell. "Isn't your study interdepartmental?"

I was feeling the intern's pressure to dispose of patients any way I could, either by transferring them to another service or via hospital discharge. Death freed up the same space as a cure, but I didn't think it was acceptable for an intern to openly wish for the death of a difficult patient. When a patient was subtracted from my list, the relief it brought me was temporary; the next patient added was likely to be just as difficult. If I didn't discharge anyone, my list would grow quickly as new abominations were added to the ones I already had. In order to maintain a small list, some clever interns became skilled at discharging only on days when they weren't on call. These interns were cursed and admired by the on-call interns, who were forced to admit patients to the beds that had opened up. Only Rulo lacked a logical replacement, since he didn't have a bed and wasn't listed in the official hospital register. If I could somehow lose Rulo, no intern would suffer for it.

Dr. Kell closed his notebook.

"We could tell psych he's on the window ledge," I suggested.

"Attending rounds tomorrow at ten. Good luck with your on-call."

"Wait," Sal said. "What should I do?"

Dr. Kell left the dayroom.

Rulo said, "If Kell and I are both on the window ledge, then I promise you, one of us is going off."

Sal laughed harshly. "Kell's a jerk. He doesn't teach us. He spends his time recording every squeak the patient makes for some bullshit protocol. What an attending."

I went to one of the large dayroom windows and forced it open, exerting all my strength against the rusty latch. Outside, it was a hot, muggy morning. Alongside Bellevue's shore, *the bedless* sunned themselves. The roar of cars sounded like the roar of waves.

"Who will be my physician?" Rulo asked. "My problem eludes all the usual investigations, all attempts at the standard cure."

Sal approached him.

"Tell me," Sal said, and Rulo, seeming delighted at the sudden interest, pointed at once to his buttocks.

"It festers, taking me over piece by rotting piece. I am changing from flesh entirely to purulence. It is my greatest humiliation. Must I beg for a bed? You see, the caretakers will not tend to a patient without a room. Such as I am, this is how I remain."

Sal backed away. The awful wound must have convinced him that treating this patient wasn't the way to improve his standing in the hospital.

"Who will help me?"

"I am assigned to your care," I said sadly. "You know that."

"May I trust you?"

"I am sworn to keep your confidence. I am your intern."

Rulo lowered his voice to a whisper. "It owns the deepest recesses of the buttocks. It is a sewer of the greenest kind of dripping, a horrid pool of microscopic creatures that multiply."

"A decubitus," I said.

"Well, medically it bears such a name. But to reduce it to a simple Latin demarcation is to denude it of the creeping agony that threatens the inner essence of my being."

"Oh come on, Mr. Rulo," Sal said. "It's a goddamn decubitus. Levy will fix it."

Rulo was incredulous. "Really? Dr. Levy can fix it?"

My time on call was taken up by small tasks. I supplemented potassium. I replaced leaking IVs that should have been changed the day before. I performed an EKG on every sleeping patient the nurses said didn't look right. Nurses paged me obsessively; the slightest sniffle was a reason to page Dr. Levy. Each intern had a different rapport with each nurse; some interns were revered, others were teased, still others were tortured. I didn't flirt, nor was I a star intern whose deft medical moves commanded instant respect. The nurses didn't seem to trust me. I made them nervous, so they tortured me. They all knew that my on-call had been deliberately moved back to Sunday.

Sal spent most of the day in the doctors' station, sleeping with his head in his hands. I tried to rouse him several times, but each time he pushed me away. One of the nurses eyed him from the hallway. She brought him a cup of coffee, which grew cold beside him. Later she returned with a plate of homemade peanut butter cookies. I ate several of the cookies and drank the cold coffee while Sal continued to sleep. His beeper was silent the entire day. He refused to accompany me on my rounds. I carried the double load myself, all the time wondering where Goldman was. Each time the emergency room notified me of a new admission, the patient had already been seen by the resident. The handwriting in the patient's chart revealed the resident's identity—author of the history and physical and the list of chores for me to complete—the enormous yet invisible Fat Goldman.

I had never felt so shunned, so humiliated, and yet I held to the tiny security of knowing that somewhere Goldman was looking over things; if anything really went wrong, he could be there to take charge. In the meantime, I didn't dare page him. My work seemed endless. An intern was a strange creature trapped inside Bellevue's concrete walls; desperate to go outside to the coffee truck, but afraid to miss the next beeper page. The nurses' pages came every five minutes, or so it seemed. The day became night and then day again without usual punctuating events like sleep or food.

Sometime during the night, Sal disappeared from the doctors' station. The nurse who'd baked the cookies told me that Sal had gone into the on-call rooms. I intended to follow him in there, but page after page interfered.

At 1 A.M. one of the patients I was covering died. His diagnosis was rule out cancer. He'd been signed over to me as "improved," despite his milk-colored skin and his low blood pressure. Because of the Do Not Resuscitate order, I didn't attempt to compensate for his failing circulation with medications. When he died, I paged Goldman, but he didn't answer my page. I was unable to locate a next of kin, and in the early morning the nurses wrapped the body in a plastic body bag and took it away to the morgue.

Early Monday morning I circled the medical floor, drawing the first of the day's bloods. I passed from patient to patient like a vampire. I began on one side of the ward and ended on the other side. Rulo's blood remained a secret. Perhaps it was incompatible with life. The nurses recorded his blood pressure in the blood pressure book as one hundred twenty over eighty, the essence of normal. But what nurse was really examining him? Larcombe's blood pressure was also one-twenty over eighty in the book. Did Larcombe have a measurable blood pressure? Pre-rounding involved ignoring these fictitious vital signs and checking to make sure the patients were still alive. An intern's worst nightmare was to find one of his patients dead in bed on resident rounds.

I was post-call. I couldn't focus my eyes. I longed for sleep, and when it became clear I didn't have time for sleep, I longed for a shower. I'd brought a change of underwear with me the day before. If only I had fifteen free minutes, I could wash and change clothes, creating a break between yesterday and today. If only I could feel fresher for an hour, perhaps the sleeplessness wouldn't overwhelm me. But I was too far behind in my work to take a shower break. The other interns were already back in the hospital. They smiled when they passed me in the hall, recognizing my condition. I had accidents drawing blood. I spilled a tube of The Biter's blood on my pants, and the stain grew large.

Across the river, University Hospital had blood-drawing and intravenous teams. University supposedly had vacuum chutes that sucked away sampled blood and brought it down to labs that no doctor ever saw. A flick of the computer light pen across the screen instantly brought the whirr of the X-ray machine, headed for the patient's room. Interns at University Hospital were rumored to sleep through the night, their work completed by modern science.

Rulo said that Bellevue also had chutes, only they were used to send incurable patients back down to the emergency room, which Rulo called The Hades. Was Rulo's mind affected by a single dose of the red liquid? In his hallucinatory view, the medical ward was Purgatory One and the *virus* ward on the top floor of the hospital was Purgatory Two. Rulo said the *virus* beds were held to the walls by hidden wires. Cutting the wires sent the afflicted hurtling down a hidden chute. Rulo said the *virus* ward was filled with the victims of *virus* bites. These doomed patients were entered into a special study of Dr. Kell's. When the study was completed, their wires were severed, and down they went.

At 8 A.M., Fat Goldman arrived at the chart rack. Our team was waiting for him. Sal stood across from him, defiantly banging his empty clipboard against his leg every few seconds. Sal hadn't changed his clothes from the day before, and he had removed his tie. He appeared tired and anxious. In contrast, Bruce and Michael looked eager and well rested. Their short white coats had been cleaned and starched. Delia also wore a white coat without creases, and her perfume smelled expensive.

I smelled of my sweat. Lab slips and X-ray request forms fell from my clipboard to the ground. As I bent down to pick them up, I felt weak and dizzy.

Goldman must have heard something about the rule out cancer patient from the night before, because he demanded an update. Before I could report on the patient's death, Sal blurted out lab results.

"A white blood count of fifty-one!" Goldman said. "What did you do about it, Levy? Did you get an X ray? Did you draw cultures? Did you call me?"

"I mean one," Sal said. "The white count was really only one."

"You ignored neutropenia in a cancer patient?"

"All cancer patients have white counts of one," Sal said.

"Bullshit. That's false. When you don't know something, ask. Notify the resident."

"Why?" Sal said sarcastically. "You mean you'd actually go with us to see a patient?"

"I tried to call you all night," I said. "You didn't respond."

"I was busy," Goldman said, with a glance at Delia. "You should have kept trying."

"Levy worked the patient up himself," Sal said. "Now the patient's fine."

"No he isn't," I corrected.

"What?!" said Goldman.

"He died."

"Another Vertino death."

"You told the interns not to sign anyone out to Vertino," I corrected.

"That was unofficially. Officially, this was still a Vertino patient."

"Look," I said. "The patient had cancer. He had a Do Not Resuscitate order. It's no one's responsibility."

"Vertino's accountable," Goldman insisted. "The patient died, and Sal didn't even know it. Just like with Ryan."

"Ryan didn't die."

"I want her back," Vertino said. "She's asked for me, and her new intern is willing to give her up. She's my patient."

Everyone laughed. I couldn't tell if the medical students agreed with Goldman or just liked kowtowing to his authority. Rulo's warning about Kell seemed absurd in the face of Goldman's growing mistreatment. Kell wasn't pulling these strings. Goldman was crushing us on his own.

A nurse came to the chart rack and informed Goldman that an intravenous line I'd replaced the night before had fallen out of the patient's vein. I was fighting an unwinnable battle.

"This is all bullshit," Sal said, nearly toppling the chart rack in his fury. "Give me back my patients."

"No way."

"Then I quit."

"Sal."

"Stay out of this, Levy."

Sal looked to Delia, but she was staring at Goldman. Sal threw off his lab coat and slammed his stethoscope to the ground.

"I quit."

"This is just what he wants you to do."

"Shut up, Levy," Goldman growled. "You'll be next."

Goldman seemed startled. It clearly wasn't the loss of

manpower that bothered him; Goldman had brought Sal down so low that he wasn't contributing. And Goldman seemed convinced that Sal was a danger to the patients and would never improve enough to be safe. But even Goldman must not have expected Sal to quit so suddenly.

For a moment I thought Sal was going to attack Goldman.

"Fuck you, pig," he said instead, and left the chart rack.

Goldman ordered Sal not to leave. Goldman watched Delia carefully, as if he were afraid that Sal's grandstanding could win her back. But Delia didn't seem affected.

"If you leave now, we won't take you back," Goldman declared.

Sal kept on walking.

"You can't do this," I said to Goldman.

"I didn't do anything. He quit."

"Sal!" I called down the hall.

"Face it. He doesn't have what it takes."

"How would you know? You never gave him a chance! You squashed him."

"I said you'll be next if you don't watch it."

"Fine. Go ahead. Fire me. See the patients yourself."

I glared at Goldman. He glared back. I knew he wouldn't fire me. He probably didn't have the authority to fire an intern, and even if he did, he wouldn't risk it without first lining up a new chump.

Bruce and Michael, though hardly Vertino advocates, seemed upset by his leaving. They stared at the floor. Delia was occupied looking through a patient's chart.

"Rounds are over," Goldman announced, though once again rounds had never really started. He tapped Delia on the shoulder, and they left the chart rack together. The vertical dance of her buttocks seemed to be a deliberate show. Bruce and Michael weren't watching. Now they were the ones examining patient charts, as if normalcy could somehow be restored by work.

But I couldn't work until I convinced Sal to come back. If I accomplished this, then I would go over Goldman's head and Kell's head and speak to The Boss. Sal needed patients. He needed guidance and reassurance. With a different resident, he could succeed. The Boss was the chief of medicine, and more than that, he was the dean of the medical school and the head of the entire Bellevue/University operation. He had absolute power.

I picked up Sal's stethoscope and lab coat and followed Goldman and Delia down the hall. Through the grease-covered windows of the dayroom, the river appeared to have spots. A Monday morning housekeeping memo promising industrial-strength cleaning was posted to the wall. Patients in wheelchairs were circled around a table. The Biter was dealing cards, his long chin thrusting forward. He dealt a poker hand to an empty space beside him.

Rulo sat with his back to me, opposite The Biter. "You cheating fang," Rulo said to The Biter. "You limping crouch. Stalking the halls for a morsel!"

The Biter exhibited his prodigious front teeth.

How did Rulo know that I was behind him? "Good morning, Dr. Levy," he said as I tiptoed past.

* * *

I looked for Sal through all the medical wards, but I couldn't find him. I paged him, but he didn't answer. I called his apartment and left a message on his answering machine. In the hope that he might still be somewhere in the hospital, I extended my search to the nonmedical wards, descending floor by floor. Twenty minutes later, I reached the rehab floor.

Fat Goldman leaned over the pool table in the middle of the rehab recreation room, calmly practicing his pool shots. In between shots he smoked a cigarette and guzzled soda from his container. He showed no remorse over the morning's events. "What about Sal?" I said. Goldman ignored me, showing off his shots for Delia, who also ignored me.

I stood there for several minutes, shifting uneasily. Rulo wheeled into the room. I looked at him with irritation. How did he know where to find me?

"I don't want this patient anymore!" I shouted at Goldman. Goldman laughed as Rulo took Sal's stethoscope from my lab coat pocket and put it around his neck. With the earpieces in his ears, Rulo searched his chest with the bell, listening for the sound of his heart.

"Shit!" he exclaimed.

"Get him out of here!"

"He's your patient. You handle him," Goldman said.

"What are you going to do about Sal?"

"He made the decision. What can I do?"

"Ten dollars a point. I'll spot you ten points to start," the living textbook said to Delia, who smiled.

"Out!" I said.

"How about twenty a point? You know, it is so airy here in Purgatory Three. So delightfully breathy. The Hades's air is fouled by death. Rue the gurneys with their captive passengers floating down the black river. Here it is the white light, the hope of re-creation. Consider the books here. Consider the music."

Rulo pointed to a bookshelf that contained several mildewed books as well as a dust-covered phonograph.

"Thirty a point and that's final," he said.

I grabbed the back of his wheelchair and began to push him from the room. He struggled, using his walking stick as a brake. Supposedly, he was wheelchair bound. Why did he have a walking stick with a black eight ball for a knob?

Delia moved in front of the wheelchair, stopping me.

"Forty," she said.

She went to the pool rack and removed a cue stick. She took off her lab coat and turned up the sleeves of her blouse. I retreated angrily to the wall. Rulo wheeled to the table, working his walking stick back and forth between his gnarly fingers.

"Too small," Delia said evenly.

"It's regulation." Rulo began to shoot with his walking stick, sinking double and triple bank shots in corner pockets. He was the ultimate wheelchair hustler. Delia laughed at him through a cloud of Goldman's cigarette smoke. Even Goldman seemed intrigued by Rulo's prowess.

Rulo attempted a quadruple bank shot. The ball went into the side pocket, followed by the cue ball.

"Shit!" Rulo exclaimed.

"Your turn," Goldman said to Delia.

"Delia," Sal Vertino said. He stood in the doorway. His arms were folded together, his legs spread apart.

Delia didn't look at anyone. She put her cue stick back in the rack and removed her lab coat from a chair. Then she walked toward the doorway. What was she thinking? How could she go from one to the other and back again in such a short time with seemingly no conscience? The men themselves alternated between pleasure and pain, their emotions fragmented, their lives disordered. Goldman would survive it. He had his career successes to tide him over until he regained control of himself. Sal was losing everything.

"You're finished, Vertino," Goldman snarled.

"He can't threaten you, Sal," I said. "He has to let you stay."

"They've got you, David," Sal said to me. "They've always had you. And they always will."

As Delia reached the doorway, Sal tried to grab her and hold her. But she pushed him back and slipped past him. He followed her into the hall.

"Delia!" Goldman shouted. "Come back here!"

"The game is not simply ended," Rulo said. "I was winning!" He rubbed his long nose. "There are well-established rules for sportsmanship. One cannot just abdicate in the middle of a match. These guidelines have been irrevocably established. One must consider them. This behavior violates common etiquette. This game is forty dollars a point!"

Goldman didn't pursue them. Perhaps he was afraid of being physically attacked by Sal. Instead, Goldman seemed to be trying to calm himself. He turned on the phonograph. He puffed on his cigarette and wiped his eyes as a blues tune scratched from the speakers.

I didn't know if Sal ever got home that night. I telephoned his apartment repeatedly, but there was no answer, and the answering machine no longer picked up. I'd been awake for forty hours already, but I couldn't sleep. How many nights could I survive like this? On-call mandated no sleep. Post-call and pre-call, sleep seemed mandatory. I feared the effects of staying awake much longer. But thoughts kept recurring: *They had me, I was the one in the vise. He was the one who was free*. The worse things became for Sal, the more he criticized my compromises. I was very angry at him. Yet I sat next to the telephone in my apartment, anxiously awaiting his call. Outside, it was raining, a hard rain that pelted the windows like hail. After several hours, I slept fitfully. I dreamed Sal and I were back in his convertible, going north. Approaching the turnoff for the Saw Mill River Parkway, Sal veered over lanes all the way to the right until we were riding on the shoulder. At the turnoff, we broke through the guardrail, flying up into the air, heading for the wall of the overpass embankment. The impact broke all the unbreakable glass. But the wall was unaffected. In the scrub grass surrounding the highway, splinters of unbreakable glass glistened. The grass grew wet with the fall of a sudden rain.

The scene shifted, and I stood with Sal on a Bellevue balcony. His nostrils were flaring as he chortled, snorting air. The sky grew lighter as the dark clouds began to move apart.

"Fuck them all. I'll dive."

"You can't do this."

Sal said that no balcony was too high. Across the river, University Hospital seemed like a mirage, shimmering in the sudden light.

"They've destroyed me. They'll kill you too. You have to get out of the trap while there's still time."

"You're paranoid," I said to dream Vertino.

"I've lost everything. You'll see. She'll leave you too."

"Sal. Don't go."

He grimaced, showing me his perfect dream teeth. "What kind of friend are you, Levy? What exactly are you up to?"

"Sal!" I yelled, as he climbed onto the railing. Would his best jump clear *the bedless,* the highway, and make it all the way to the river? A gorgeous jackknife dive, followed by a champion stroke, swimming away forever?

He was over the railing.

Below us, white stretchers were covered with *the bedless*. One left his stretcher to kneel by the river. "We're poor. Poor us. Pour us another," a *bedless* by the river seemed to say.

When I looked again, a large sailboat was coming down the river. It was practically a schooner. Its sails were full open to the wind, and it was moving at a prodigious clip. Was that Sal swimming up to it, hauling himself on board without the sailboat even slowing down?

I left the balcony and entered the patient's room. The covers were drawn up over her head, and I knew she was no longer just sleeping. As I pulled the covers back, the sun rose over a rain cloud and lit her face. A pale blue color had replaced her color of a moment before, when at her sickest, her most lifeless, she was still called life. Now she was acquiring the stiffness that was beyond all maneuvering.

"Bone is bone," I said, but no one replied. Down below me, by the river, *the bedless* seemed to be mouthing her name.

"Mrs. Ryan," I called to her, and then I awoke.

5

The telephone was ringing. I picked up the receiver, and a mechanical voice informed me that I'd won countless prizes and was eligible for trips to far-off lands. As a bonus, I was being sent a carton of condoms that were guaranteed to provide protection against *the virus.*

"How about a partner?" I said, but the mechanical voice made no further offer.

I hung up and checked my watch. It was six o'clock. The rain had stopped. The sky and river were metallic blue, the color of a Chevy Impala. The sun had begun its climb through the lower sky with the ease of Rulo moving through Bellevue Hospital.

I showered and dressed quickly, feeling stiff and lethargic from lack of sleep. I returned to Bellevue just before seven o'clock. I knew I had to work, though I couldn't stop thinking of Sal. I tried to interpret my dream. What was the meaning of the sailboat? One thing was certain, Sal was in danger. My dream revealed that the more he was risking himself, the more uncertain he became. All the near misses driving with Sal had forged their way into my unconscious, until an accident seemed imminent. And everything in Sal's world, including the few patients he'd begun to care about, seemed to be in jeopardy.

But Mrs. Ryan was still alive. She was sitting in her bed, eating the liquiefied powder the food service called eggs. Eating increased her shortness of breath. In between forkfuls, she pursed her lips with the austerity of a chronic lunger. She seemed angered by my presence.

"Why are you here?"

I couldn't tell her my dream. I bowed my head, signaling an apology for intruding, and left the room.

"Where's Dr. Vertino?!" she shouted after me.

I pre-rounded, beginning with Sal's patients. It was important to maintain them in as good a condition as possible. If Sal returned to full duty, he couldn't be overwhelmed right away.

The nurses informed me that The Biter had assaulted Larcombe during the night. Today, The Biter was tied to the side rails of his bed. His stringy hair drooped down over his narrow nose and chin. Drool spilled from his mouth and formed large brown globs on his pillow. Larcombe was missing from the room, though the nurses insisted he hadn't been sent anywhere for a test.

"Where's Mr. Larcombe?" I asked The Biter.

He opened his mouth and let out more drool. He remained quiet while I drew his blood. Was he sated from a recent meal? As I jabbed him with the needle and he flinched, I felt a distinct pleasure. I was tempted to use a larger needle, to assault him again more invasively. He was a likely target for my anger. He was despicable and clearly deserving of punishment. But I wasn't his judge. I wasn't entitled to inflict him with unnecessary pain. In fact, when I was through drawing his blood and was backing away from his bed, I suddenly felt embarrassed.

I was growing more restless, despite my intention to be thorough. I completed my pre-rounds as quickly as possible, listening to hearts and lungs with the dispatch of an attending. When I was finished, I glanced through the charts, then went to the on-call rooms with twenty minutes still remaining before rounds.

The main door to the on-call rooms lacked a doorknob. Instead, there was a hole in the door and a thick piece of wire slung through it. The first week there had been a memo from maintenance promising repair, but this week the memo was gone.

Beyond the main door, a long hallway led into the common room. Here the outer walls were lined with lockers and the thin-walled cubicles intended to serve on-call doctors as bedrooms.

Goldman's papers were piled high on a four-foot couch at the center of the common room—Xeroxes of journal articles, travel brochures, out-of-date schedules. On Friday, the other chief residents had removed these papers from their office by hand truck and dumped them here, an obvious slight. If Goldman's contemporaries were using his assignment to our wretched team as an excuse to dishonor him, it was bound to make Goldman even angrier at us. But I was happy to see Sal's abuser punished. Could the other chiefs possibly hate Goldman as much as we did?

A paper sign absurdly designated the on-call rooms as Goldman's new office. He could rule us from his monarchical couch, distributing his Xeroxes. "Calcium Metabolism and Blood Dyscrasias" was at the top of the pile, covered with stains and candy bar goop and ready for distribution. "Tuberculosis in Health Care Workers" was on the floor, gray with a dozen intern footprints.

I was alone in the on-call rooms. The other interns were out on the wards, working. I stood before Sal's locker. His lock was gone; his locker was empty. Suddenly I felt a great remorse. He had no intention of returning, and there was nothing I could do about it. How different things might have been if only we'd been given a different resident to supervise us.

"What are you doing here?" a woman's voice said, and

footsteps sounded in the hall. "You're supposed to be working."

Delia came down the hall and into the common room. She sat on Goldman's couch, prying a half-empty two-liter container out from between the cushions. This was the first time I could recall being alone with her. I watched her closely; wondering if my expression revealed how much I despised her. She seemed to be trying to flirt with me. She played with the container, rolling it back and forth between her hands. She squeezed the plastic into a dent, then played it back out until the dent was gone.

A bare lightbulb dimly lit the room. Our shadows mixed behind the couch. I smelled my sweat together with her perfume.

"Where's Sal?"

She smirked. "Doesn't he tell you where he's going?"

I suppressed a sudden urge to grab her by the neck.

"Stop the bullshit. Where's Sal?"

She left the couch abruptly and went into the corner cubicle. She turned on the light, and I saw a woman's black leather coat on the flimsy bed. She picked up the coat and put it around her shoulders. She moved freely in the room as though she were an intern.

"You're not supposed to be in there."

She slammed the door to the cubicle and locked it from inside.

I was about to bang on the door and insist she open it, when my pager went off, a shrill toll echoing in the quiet. It almost seemed as if Delia had willed it to go off.

The telephones in the on-call rooms weren't working. No memo promised repair. I was paged a second time. I went back out to the doctors' station to answer it. When the page operator didn't respond after nineteen rings, I dialed STAT page, a maneuver that caused huge bells to clang in the operators' tiny switchboard room downstairs. After four of these monumental rings, a sleepy voice said hello. Since I couldn't justify using STAT page, I hung up. Perhaps now she would answer the regular line. After twenty rings, she finally did answer, and she told me that Dr. Goldman was looking for me.

"I've paged you four times," he said when we were connected. "Where the fuck are you?"

"This is the first page I've received. I'm in the doctors' station. Where are you? Where are rounds?"

"Forget rounds. A patient needs you down in emergency."

"A new patient? But I'm not on call."

Goldman hung up the phone.

In the emergency room alcove where the clerks stockpiled supplies, a *bedless* woman slept on a stretcher. She wore a heavy coat and at least two sweaters. Did she suffer from chills, or was she accumulating clothing for the winter? Would she announce her desolation to me in exchange for a few coins? Her stretcher was wheel-deep in feculent water. A drainage pipe had burst, turning the entire emergency room into a swamp. A memo from housekeeping was taped to the wall of the alcove. I didn't bother to read it. I was furious, thinking this was the patient Goldman meant. If he assigned me a new patient when I wasn't on call, he was bringing my punishment to yet another level.

A bearded clerk wearing rubber boots approached me from across the room.

"This isn't your patient, Dr. Levy. Your patient is on the other side."

"Where is Dr. Goldman?"

"How should I know. I just work here. I don't keep tabs on doctors."

He splashed through the ridiculous water, leading me to a stretcher where Larcombe lay, unmoving. He looked ill, even for Larcombe. His curly hair was soaked, as if he'd floated into the ER through the broken sewer pipe.

"How did he get here? He has a bed upstairs."

"They found him outside. He looked hungry, so they brought him in."

"He can't eat. He has a feeding tube."

"You're his doctor. You want to feed him through a tube, go ahead. I'm telling you, the guy's been eating sandwiches all morning."

"That's bullshit."

"You can't talk to me like that," the clerk said. "I'll report you."

"Go ahead. Fucking report me!"

"Tomorrow. Right now my shift is over."

The clerk splashed away.

On a cart near the stretcher there was a pile of unwrapped cheese sandwiches on stale white bread. I took a sandwich and angrily stuffed it into Larcombe's mouth.

His mouth began to move, and he made chewing sounds. For a moment he seemed sentient.

"Lousy sandwich," he said.

"What did you say?"

Larcombe stared at the ceiling, smiling blankly.

Thinking I might be delirious, I went outside to the coffee truck and bought a cup of coffee. The morning wind was pushing the clouds eastward. The sun shone directly on Bellevue.

A rope of sheets hung from Larcombe's window to the ground. Could he possibly have made the rope himself and used it to escape from The Biter?

The bedless sat on their stretchers by the river and ate sandwiches. The light cast long shadows and caused them to appear misshapen. Was one twitching with the clonus of an undiagnosed dystrophy?

I leaned against the outer wall of Bellevue. My pager sounded, but I ignored it. I thought of Delia, inside the cubicle, perhaps preparing for her next visitor. She went from one to the other. She was attentive only to her current choice. If she knew where Sal was, she didn't seem to care, and she certainly wasn't going to tell me. Delia hoarded information like she hoarded people, still possessing even as she lost interest.

The sheet rope billowed up in a sudden gust of wind. A moment later, Delia and Goldman stepped out onto Larcombe's balcony and went to the railing. Goldman stood behind her, his bulk pressing against her back. He pointed to the sheet trail, and I thought I saw him laugh. Larcombe's bizarre sojourn in the ER had been a convenient excuse to get me out of the way.

"Some emergency," I said aloud.

Goldman looked down over the railing. I was sure he could see me, but he was too far away to have heard what I said.

They never showed up at the chart rack for rounds. One of the other chief residents came. He informed me and a frowning Bruce and Michael that Dr. Goldman had gotten sick with a sudden virus and gone home. The chief resident looked angry, and I doubted he believed Goldman's story. But when I started to complain, he silenced me with a wave of his hand and walked away. The other chiefs definitely didn't want to be involved in our mess. Once again, no one rounded with us. Dr. Kell didn't come, despite his promise.

That evening, I was on my way out of the hospital when I saw The Boss walking down the hall. I followed him. He was dressed in a thirty-year-old suit, and he walked with the halting gait of advancing age. His hair was white and fluffed up like a cotton wig. Despite his stature as a great medical leader, few at Bellevue appeared to recognize him, and no one stopped to greet him. He seemed uncomfortable and out of place. Two ragpickers brushed past him, exchanging hidden contraband from hand to hand.

The Boss was far removed from the chief residents and even from Kell. Well past seventy, he still wielded great power and could control anyone's career if he felt like it. He was, after all, still chief of medicine, and beyond that, the head of the entire medical center, Bellevue and University Hospital, combined. He was said to prefer Bellevue because he saw it as the place for teaching. He kept his offices here. University Hospital was the place for money making, a preoccupation The Boss derided. At Bellevue, The Boss watched students grow into doctors. Unfortunately, rewarding his favorite residents with promotion often meant seeing them turn into money-coveting attendings at University Hospital.

From the start of Sal's troubles, I'd been thinking of appealing directly to The Boss. The rumor was that he was demented, that he advertised in the *Times* every month for an android body. Was he too demented to help Sal? The Boss's greatest critics still feared his wrath, and they remained jealous of his power. They had more motivation for being insidious that he had. Maybe I could still appeal to his humanity. It was generally considered impossible to get past his secretaries. No one would expect me to be able to reach him. Encountering him in the hall like this was a sudden lucky chance. If I complained about Goldman or Kell, The Boss probably wouldn't listen to me. My best chance was to plead for Sal directly. If I could persuade The Boss to give Sal another chance, Goldman and Kell would have to abide by the decision.

I approached him just before the incline in the hallway that led to Bellevue's exit. The Boss nodded when he saw me. Still, I suspected he didn't know me. It was too easy for an intern to misinterpret that familiar nod as meaning the intern was favored or in trouble.

"Dr. Bruner," I said, and The Boss stopped walking.

I didn't know what to say first. Was it best to refer to his favorite sport, baseball, or to offer encouraging words about his recently fractured toe? When something happened to The Boss, it was an immediate source of gossip around Bellevue.

He spoke first. "I'm sorry about your friend," he said in a slow, heavy voice. "What do you think we can do about it?"

I was stunned, but I recovered quickly. The Boss was an unexpected ally. "Bring him back, Dr. Bruner. Encourage him to come back. You know how hard it is here with minimal staffing and support services. On top of that, people have deliberately antagonized him. But Sal could turn into the best kind of intern. If only he could receive the right attention. He cares about his patients. He's a hard worker."

The Boss seemed to understand.

"Back when I was an intern, we had a portable X-ray machine that was so faulty it gave me an electric shock whenever I tried to use it. No one cared enough about the interns to get rid of it or buy a new one. Finally, I wheeled it out of the hospital and dumped it under the new highway. You know, it's still out there to this day. My resident didn't know whether to throw me out of the program or call me a hero."

"But Dr. Bruner. This is about more than just equipment. It's Sal's life."

I was fatigued beyond being sleepless, and too angry to be polite. But The Boss didn't appear insulted that I hadn't accepted his cocktail-party story as equivalent to Sal's experience. At the same time, the sheepish expression he used as a mask dissolved into a sudden knowing look.

"All right. He stays on service. If you can convince him to come back, he stays. Just keep him out of any more trouble."

The Boss lifted his hand upward, a gesture I interpreted as deferring to a power over which even he had no control. Then he pushed open the glass exit door and walked out to the street.

That night it was raining again. I walked under an umbrella to Sal's apartment. He lived on the bottom floor of a brownstone only three blocks from the hospital. The literature professor who owned it was now overseas in Europe and wasn't expected back until the spring. I had no idea what arrangement she was expecting with Sal when she returned.

The street seemed to belong to a quieter, more remote neighborhood than I expected to find this close to Bellevue. The apartment building was covered in ivy and shaded by sycamore trees. Copies of Monday's and Tuesday's *Times* were rolled up on the wet stoop, the rubber band still around them. I knocked at the front door and rang the doorbell, but there was no answer. I tried the doorknob, which turned, so I opened the door and went inside.

In the living room, floor-to-ceiling bookshelves were filled with worn copies of old English novels and books of poetry. Sal's clothes and his medical books were scattered on the floor. A new edition of *Harrison's Internal Medicine*, still in its bookstore cellophane, lay on the mantel. In the fireplace, ashes and partially burned logs remained from past fires. I felt the ashes and found them cool.

I went into the kitchen. The sink was filled with dishes and the remains of partially eaten food. Despite the food, there wasn't a smell. The window was open, and rain wet the windowsill. On the square wooden table, a melting stick of butter had a knife halfway through it. Sunday's newspaper, without a rubber band, lay folded up on a chair.

I reconstructed the events—Sal had last been here early Monday morning. He'd gone to the hospital and quit his residency, throwing away the long years of sacrifice and preparation. Then he'd gone to the poolroom and confronted Delia. By Monday night, Sal had disappeared. By Tuesday, Delia was enjoying the balcony view with Fat Goldman.

As an intern, I was experiencing a slowdown of events for the first time since early childhood. Everything was new, absorbed by a willing sponge; great amounts of learning were packed into twenty-four-hour periods that each seemed to last a month. The result was a new identity for me as a doctor. Even without proper guidance or rounds, I was becoming a dispenser of care. I served the vulnerable while living the illusion of being beyond harm myself. But Sal was devolving in the opposite direction. The risk of harm was growing by the day as his life unraveled. Large pieces of his identity and his sense of prowess were disintegrating. I felt a great sadness and impotence. The evidence was here in his apartment with all its objects in disarray. There was no joy or hope to be conjured here.

Wednesday morning, neither Delia nor Goldman showed up for work. I probably would have enjoyed the calm direction of the replacement resident, if only I'd known where Sal was. I worried about him all day. The phone at his apartment rang on and on without an answering machine to stop it. I pleaded with the Bellevue operator to connect me long distance to Giuseppe's clinic, but when she finally agreed, no one answered there, either. At the hospital, the interns and residents didn't want to talk about Sal. The nurses no longer peeked into the doctors' station, hoping to find him. It was as if everyone had already forgotten that he'd ever been at Bellevue.

Thursday, I was scheduled to be on call again, nevertheless, Wednesday night I decided it was time to return to Catskill. I didn't believe that the clinic was closed, though the phone there continued to ring without answer.

I hated to drive my old Toyota. "Turn the key and who knows?" Sal always said, preferring to ride in his Alfa.

I drove the Toyota past Sal's empty parking place, rattling out the exit and on up the street to the highway entrance ramp. The old car whirred and lurched, its rusty engine cylinders catching, then missing. The radio played static in a rhythm established by the missing cylinders. I traveled north on the wet highway, past the exit for the bridge to Queens. Air whistled into the Toyota through holes in the floorboard. I stayed in the right lane, the retread tires hugging the shoulder. The rain had stopped again sometime during the day, and now the sky was clearing. As I drove I regained my hope. I would find Sal in Catskill and convince him to return to the program with The Boss's benediction.

I took the exit for the Major Deegan Expressway. Twenty minutes later, I reached the turnoff for the Saw Mill River Parkway. I didn't take the turnoff. I hesitated, but I didn't think Sal had gone to Hastings-on-Hudson. Delia was too busy cavorting at Bellevue with Fat Goldman. Sal's "safe place" was with his grandfather. I puttered past the lights of the exit ramp, past the dark embankment of the overpass. The railing was whole. Unlike my dream, there was no glass. I gas pedaled the Toyota into its ratchety imitation of acceleration. Sal's emergency plan was to return to Catskill. The old doc's town was eighty miles ahead of me.

The land became more rural. I exited the thruway onto a tar road. A traffic light turned briefly yellow and then went red. The Toyota seemed about to break apart as I pushed on the brake and slowed it down from fifty.

I reached Catskill at ten o'clock, stopping for gas at the only station on Main Street. The young attendant manning the single pump smiled when he saw the Toyota.

"How long have you worked here?" I asked him casually.

"About a year. Why?"

"Did you know the man who died?"

He didn't answer me, but he gripped the trigger on the gas nozzle until the numbers on the meter flew. His expression was so grim, I no longer doubted Sal's witch story.

Leaving the gas station, I drove on past the Catskill Diner. Following a sign with a large H, I traveled up a short hill then down an unlit road. There was a single light in the distance. Soon there was the opening in the trees and the sign for Dr. Vertino's clinic.

I parked the Toyota on the muddy driveway next to Giuseppe's truck. I climbed the porch, opened the screen door, and went inside. A clerk was at the front desk, smoking a cigarette, sorting through papers.

"No one's been answering the phone here," I said. He didn't look up.

"I'm David. A friend of Sal's."

The clerk continued to ignore me. I headed toward the rear of the clinic.

"Sal isn't here, Dr. Levy," he called after me.

The smell of burning wood came from a fireplace in

Giuseppe's office, but a GONE FISHING sign was attached to his office door. I knew where to look for him. Just beyond the clinic, the woods resumed and a stream that was a branch off Hudson's river gurgled over mossy rocks. Trout rested in tiny pools beneath these rocks. A fly fisherman waded slowly into the stream, whipping his line onto the fertile water.

"Dr. Vertino. It's David Levy!"

"Shhh! What are you doing here?"

"Sal quit. Now I can't find him."

He was thigh-deep in the water. I slipped on the mud of the shore, unable to grip the ground with my old sneakers. Moonlight reflected back off his hip waders and his orange vest. I could see the glint on the fishing line as it was thrown, but I couldn't hear the plop of the fly over the rush of the stream. The wind seemed to be whispering in time to the fly casting, *Where's Sal? What's happening to my boy?* Giuseppe himself stayed silent, no doubt obeying the fisherman's superstition that sound would scare the fish.

The photograph on his office wall must have been taken here. A younger Giuseppe fished with his son Joe, who was college age, or maybe even medical-school age. Had Sal's father been governed by the same passions or sarcasms as Sal? Or had Joe been stronger, more like Giuseppe, dedicated to his work and uncompromising?

There was a plop. At first I thought it was a fish jumping, but then I realized that something had landed on the bank.

"It's a letter. Came today. Read it," Giuseppe shouted, breaking the code of silence.

He'd protected it from the water with a plastic wrapper. The envelope was addressed to Giuseppe, with no return address. I recognized the handwriting—the *e*'s were tight like *i*'s. The *i*'s were looped like *e*'s. The capital letters were stiff and formal, the lowercase letters were squiggles shaped like tiny serpents. I opened the envelope easily; it was no longer sealed. The letter also was handwritten. It was dated with Tuesday's date, and the writing was faint and scratchy, as though the pen were losing ink. Why was Giuseppe carrying this letter with him?

"You wanted to know," Giuseppe called to me, as I began to read.

Dear Pops,

There were those times when all you could offer was the knowledge, with no treatment for the illness. But the knowledge, you said, could also be the comfort, for the doctor, and for the patient. "We cling to it like a flashlight on a blind trail," you said. Maybe it's the reason you've kept the clinic going all these lonely years. I don't know.

I don't remember my father. No matter how many ways I try to think of him, I can't reach him. The descriptions I have of his life are meaningless. Sometimes I think my struggles are a way to find him. I mean, no Vertino ever made it through internship without a disaster, eh Pops?

I remember the clinic in winter, those crisp mornings, fishing through the ice, watching you smoke. I remember the coffee and the thick, sweet milk from the cow next door. You taught me to pasteurize. I remember the old stove we came home to. You must have known I was wishing for that stove the whole time we were out on the ice. But I never asked you to take me back. "We have our hearts to warm us," you said. We were Vertinos.

I can't do it Pops. They've beaten me. And I *am* beaten. There's only one way out of internship. Success is the only option. But I'm a failure, and there's no changing it. There's no way back for me now.

Yesterday was heavy rain, the kind you say makes your head numb when you walk around in it. The driveway at Delia's fills with mud just like the clinic's does when we park a mile away and slosh our way to work. I remember getting stuck the first time you let me drive the truck and how you had to push me out.

Pops, I need the courage to face you. There's no going back for me now.

This is Delia's house, the woman I told you about. Her father owns it, but he never comes here. No one knew I was coming here, not even Levy. I love Levy like a brother, but he doesn't understand my situation. He can't help me, and I'm not sure I can still trust him.

* * *

Giuseppe remained out on the river, fishing in the dark.

"He says I can't help him," I called, but Giuseppe didn't respond.

I continued reading the letter, growing more distressed with each line. Apparently, Sal had awoken in the middle of the night and heard Delia talking on the telephone to someone at the hospital. When he'd confronted her, she denied that it was Goldman. The following morning, Delia was gone. Sal waited for several hours for her to return. Dr. Kell called—how did Kell know where to find him, Sal wondered?—and insisted that Sal see a psychiatrist. Sal's letter ended with his growing dread and fear of Kell . . .

> He's crazy and mean and he could do anything. He could be turning into the driveway right now. What should I do? Nothing's safe for me anymore. Do I still have my strength? Or do I have *the virus?* I love you, Pops. Oh God, I'm so afraid. I'll get to you somehow. Keep the fire in the old stove burning for me.

I left the bank and slipped out into the stream, nearly falling over several rocks hidden in the dark water. It was quite cold, and my soaked pants stuck to me, making it difficult to move forward. Still, I managed to reach the middle of the stream without falling. Giuseppe was waiting. Under any other circumstances he might have been laughing at me, but instead I saw that his expression was entirely serious. He looked worried.

"Sal really thinks he loves her," he said. "He's losing himself."

"He's afraid he may have *the virus.*"

"No, he's not. Not really. He's just paranoid of everything."

How could Sal suspect me? I wondered. I was his closest friend. How believable were his suspicions when he included me in the group of his betrayers? I was terribly hurt by this, yet I wanted so much to find Sal and help bring him back. Could he still be in Hastings-on-Hudson, almost two days after this letter was written?

"The Boss told me he'll give Sal another chance."

Giuseppe shrugged at the mention of his old friend Dr. Bruner. "Sal does what he wants. I can never really influence him. No one can."

The current was stronger and the water felt colder. I began to shiver, yet I stayed where I was. The old man was no longer paying attention to his fishing. He allowed his rod to drop down as he hummed and mumbled to himself. *Come back, Sal. Start over* were the imagined whispers now in the wind. But Giuseppe was slumped over, his head and shoulders drooping down, his knees buckling and following his rod into the water.

"*Il figlio è pazzo, il figlio è perduto*"—the boy is crazy, the boy is lost—I thought I heard him say.

PART THREE

THE CRASH ROOM

July 10th

6

Driving back from Catskill, I took the thruway turnoff to Hastings-on-Hudson. I made a wrong turn that brought me miles out of my way, but eventually, I was able to find Delia's street. The electric lantern at the house on the corner wasn't lit. I was too nervous to stop, so I drove around the block. The second time around, I forced myself to pull into Delia's driveway. There were no cars parked in front of the house. I leaned on my car horn, but the muffled rasp went unanswered. I grew more afraid, dreading what I might find here.

I left the car. Climbing to the dark

porch, "Sal," I whispered, and then, louder, "Sal." My voice sounded small, absorbed by the trees and the background wash of Hudson's river.

No one answered the doorbell. I tried to open the door, but it was locked. Sal had written of me as a betrayer, but I was determined to help him. The longer I went without finding him, the more worried I became. I began to search the woods off the side of the porch, but after ten steps there was no light at all. I grew too afraid to go on.

Back in the car, I drove away as quickly as I could. I reached my apartment in the city at two o'clock in the morning. I phoned Sal's apartment without success until after three. At 3:30, I began to worry that I wouldn't be able to sleep. This was an intern's second greatest fear aside from inadvertently killing a patient—to be awake the entire night *before* an on-call.

But somehow I managed to sleep for three hours. I slept through my alarm clock, waking disoriented, staggering back to the hospital at 7:30, too late to pre-round. I arrived at the doctors' station just as Dr. Kell was removing his suit jacket and replacing it with the long white coat of a University attending. I couldn't believe it was Kell arriving for rounds. His unexpected presence seemed to be a hallucination. He adjusted his spectacles and peered at the list of patients that was taped to the wall glass of the doctors' station. He shifted back and forth, transferring his weight from one leg to the other, appearing as uncomfortable at being here as I was at seeing him.

"A covering resident will be here in an hour," he said.

"Dr. Goldman phoned in a phony excuse. He's in real trouble."

Staring at Kell, I was suddenly convinced that Sal's letter was a mistake. It was impossible to look at Kell and see the stalking ghoul that Sal described. Kell was tall and quietly confident. He dressed beautifully. His cologne was luxurious. Even his momentary nervousness was reassuring. Kell was human. I suspected that the greatest discoveries in medicine came from doctors capable of moments of self-doubt.

Kell smiled at me, and I instantly imagined relief from persecution, with Kell to teach me, Kell to guide me. How much of Sal's and now Goldman's problems came from their obsession with a sick, crazy woman? Perhaps Sal's reactions had less to do with Kell than with Sal losing his mind. To see Dr. Kell in the light of day was to see a calm, well-controlled physician at the peak of his career. Even with all the uncertainty about my friend, I began to feel hopeful for the first time in days. I was about to partake in attending rounds. I rehearsed the patients I would present to Dr. Kell. Perhaps being in the harness of real teaching would be enough to overcome a second night without sleep. Other interns were walking zombies yet remained organized, living on their resident's brain. Until now, our team had lacked the direction that other teams relied on routinely.

But my new hope faded as the minutes passed and no one else came. Our group was supposed to be on call, yet Kell and I were alone in the doctors' station. Where was the rest of our team?

"Where are the medical students?" I asked.

"They've been reassigned."

With this one statement, my expectations disappeared. It was notable *not* that Kell was here today for attending rounds, but that he hadn't been here on any of the previous days. He looked like a helping professional, but it was becoming evident that he wasn't here to help me. Whatever his motivation was, it was probably driven by self-interest. In wanting to feel better about Kell, I'd forgotten entirely about the red liquid and that it might well be harming the patients.

"We're already minus an intern. We need more manpower, not less. How can we have rounds without a full team?"

Kell sneered. "You're absolutely right. No rounds will take place."

"How am I supposed to learn anything?"

"You're also minus a patient," he said, ignoring my question. "Mr. Rulo was moved to University Hospital for special testing."

I imagined the scene through Rulo's eyes. Late at night the stretcher had arrived. Glad hands had carried Rulo away, out the back door of Bellevue, past the sleeping *bedless,* to the ambulance boat. Protesting his plight, Rulo had been brought by force across the dark river. He was to be studied by the University arm of Dr. Kell's protocol. I was sad at the departure of Bellevue's resident soothsayer. Only Rulo seemed to understand what truly motivated Kell. What new dangers awaited Rulo at University Hospital?

"Why wasn't I informed?"

Kell sneered again and pointed to the list of patients. "Forget Rulo. He's off the list. Tell me about Larcombe. Does he meet study criteria?"

"What about Rulo's decubitus? Doesn't the patient's comfort count for anything?"

Kell's eyeglasses had slipped to the last inch of his nose. He peered through them with obvious disdain.

"What counts is that we treat them and move them out."

"How can I treat them without a team?"

"Larcombe," Kell said, again ignoring my question.

"You want to know his diagnosis? He's a stroke patient, multiple infarcts."

"I don't need to know his diagnosis. I need to know is if he has any relatives. Who will sign his consent form for the study?"

Kell clearly wasn't interested in teaching me. I was just a slave for his mysterious study. The more he dismissed me, the more frustrated and angry I became. But I knew I was trapped by his authority. He remained the head of this single-member team.

"Keep Larcombe sedated," he said. "I don't want him to panic when he sees the study fluid."

"He's completely out of it. Shouldn't he be on neurology?"

"Not a chance. We have an arrangement with neurology. We never take their patients, and they never take our patients."

"What am I supposed to do for him here?"

"Nothing. That's why he isn't on the teaching service."

"But this is the teaching service."

Kell looked at me even more disdainfully. "Not anymore," he said.

Abruptly, he left the doctors' station and walked toward the patients' rooms. I followed behind him, mortified at the latest demotion. It was difficult to imagine anything more Kell could do to dismantle this team without doing away with it altogether. Every day I fell further behind the other interns. Now Kell was taking away my right to attend lectures and conferences. How was I supposed to learn the skills of being a doctor?

We toured the patients' rooms, a mockery of true attending rounds, as Kell dramatized his ideas to an imaginary audience. He waved his hands in the air and swung his stethoscope for emphasis. Ignoring actual patient complaints, he demonstrated their heart murmurs and their lung sounds, proclaiming that no other physician had better ears for the stethoscope than he had. We visited five of my patients—two with cancer, two with heart disease, and one with *the virus*. Kell probed their bodies, but he didn't introduce himself to any of them.

Two of my patients seemed perfectly healthy, and I dreaded showing them to Kell. I had no idea why these patients remained in the hospital. They never responded to direct questions about their condition. Their charts revealed no diagnoses. They were roommates, and most mornings on pre-rounds I would find them dressed, asleep in their chairs, or listening to music on their headphones. They had the only working television on the floor, and they also had a VCR.

This particular morning they wore their hospital gowns, and they slept in their beds.

"Housekeepers," Kell mumbled, standing outside the room. "Disabled members of the union. They stay here as long as they want."

Posted on the wall, there was an undated memo promising beautification: The windows would be cleaned, the floors would be washed, the walls would be painted, and new steel guardrails were going to be secured to the sides of every bed. As Kell walked away, he brushed against the wall. The memo was knocked loose and floated to the floor. I suspected it would be days before a floor-sweeping housekeeper discovered this memo on his rounds.

Kell paced the hallway. He seemed to have lost interest in manipulating bodies into unseemly postures without first asking the owners' permission. How many rashes, inflamed joints, or whooshing heart murmurs could he claim had gone undetected until he personally discovered them?

He rubbed his hands together and peered at me intently. Even before he spoke, I suddenly knew why he was here, why he had come to the doctors' station in the first place. Maybe Rulo's telepathy was contagious.

"Where is Vertino?!" he said abruptly.

Sal's letter had described it—Kell's preoccupation with finding him. Kell had come to the doctors' station looking for him. Did Kell think that if he stayed with me Sal would appear?

Kell seemed so anxious, I wondered if he were losing control of himself. I couldn't have predicted his shift of mood from his unflappable appearance. He seemed to be consumed by rage that he was generating himself.

Did The Boss know how Kell tormented us? Did The Boss know we were no longer a teaching service, that our students had been reassigned? Our patients roamed the halls and escaped out of windows. Our resident avoided us and then took leave with a feigned illness. Our attending also avoided us and then he policed us. What would The Boss say about a ward where the patients' charts were thick with months of notes, yet the patients themselves were rarely interviewed or examined?

I was paged. Kell glared at me as I went to find a phone.

"Wait," he said. "Tell me where Vertino is. I must speak to him."

Kell's unmasked need to find Sal was very disturbing. Sal had pitted himself against authority until he was ground out in defeat. But Kell seemed intent on finishing him off. Did questioning Kell's power mean initiating an impersonal sequence as devastating as a Terminator's? Or was there a more personal reason that Kell was so obsessed?

I had gone down the hall to a wall phone when Kell, seeming more agitated, caught up to me.

"The nurses are afraid of Sal," Kell said. "I must keep him away from the nurses."

"Bullshit. The nurses love him."

Was Kell jealous? Maybe my friend was right about Kell. Maybe he also had an eye for Delia.

"I have to answer this page," I said, and continued walking. I was having a Rulo-type premonition that Sal was finally calling, and I didn't want Kell to overhear me.

"Wait. I didn't dismiss you."

Defying Kell and his farce of attending rounds, I ducked into a stairway and hid behind the door. I guessed—correctly—that Kell was too proud to enter the stairs.

There was an emergency phone on the wall inside the stairwell. The receiver smelled of urine and was slippery with an unknown substance. But the phone worked, probably because the stairs were outside the domain of both housekeeping and maintenance. The page operator answered me after only twenty rings and announced that Sal Vertino was paging me.

"Where is he?"

"Emergency room."

"Connect me!"

There was a pause.

"It's too late. He's gone."

"Can't you get him back?"

"I've already told you. He's no longer on the line. Scream at me again and I'll have to report you."

I descended the stairs three at a time. The emergency room was still under water. I sloshed from one wall phone to another, but I couldn't find Sal. I grew more and more frustrated. Perhaps Sal was outside. I approached the glass doors of the entrance. My weight on the rubber mat should have triggered the doors to open. Instead, I smacked my head against the unyielding glass as I tried to go through. Beyond these doors, an ambulance drove past Bellevue with its roof lights flashing, its sirens blaring. It didn't stop or even slow down. It was moving like an express train past a station.

After several unsuccessful attempts to get outside, I flopped down in defeat on an unwashed stretcher in the outermost stretcher bay. Here the stench of festering wounds and filthy clothes and bodies competed with the presiding odor of the sewer water. A housekeeping sign promising to FUMIGATE AND CLEAN was posted on the wall across from me. Many of the patients here had severe lung, skin, or kidney infections, yet they awaited beds upstairs for hours, sometimes even for days. When a bed finally became available, it couldn't receive a new patient until a housekeeper had been found to change the sheets.

It was difficult to tell stretcher-bay patients apart from *the bedless*. In fact, *the bedless* often insinuated themselves among the infected, eating their sandwiches, drinking their coffee, borrowing their blankets.

In the middle of this group of patients, a man in a business suit lay on his back with his shirtsleeve ripped open and an IV taped to his arm. The victim of a sudden illness that had caused his unconditional surrender to the city ambulance, he complained bitterly and loudly about his predicament.

"Take me to the University," he bellowed to everyone who passed him.

Strangely, it wasn't the filth or the stench that caused

me to get up from the stretcher where I lay. Listening to the businessman complain, I regained my resolve. He was so irritating, I felt compelled to move away from him and resume my search for Sal.

Farther inside the ER, there was a second large stretcher bay. Aides wheeled stretchers past here at great speeds, on their way to the innermost rooms. They seemed ready to trample anyone who strayed into their path.

The stretchers of the second alcove were crowded close together. The patients had sheets pulled up to the tops of their heads, and I couldn't be sure that they were only sleeping. Two stretchers were parked side by side in the corner. One patient was motionless, and the other dripped a fluid, probably a medication leaking from an intravenous unit. The drop-by-drop descent reminded me of drool. The patient shifted on the stretcher as if to set himself apart from his inert neighbor. As the patient moved, his feet came out from under the sheet and gave away his identity; I saw the familiar sneakers and then I saw the curls of black hair sticking out from under the sheet at the head of the gurney and flattening against the wall of the alcove.

I was so happy to see him that I lost all perspective and considered bringing him a doctor's white coat. Perhaps he could resume working shortly.

Unfortunately, the physician's operative illusion of being beyond harm didn't apply to Sal. He was delirious. He didn't seem to recognize me. The clipboard on the side of the stretcher listed his temperature as 105, which meant it could really be as high as 108. He appeared to be suffering from a septic condition. Unless his diagnosis became certain, he would be a rule out patient: rule out *the virus*, rule out tuberculosis, rule out Bellevue bacteria.

Two days before, he'd written the letter to his grandfather while stranded on Delia's porch. Had he given up hope of her return, wandering off confused and defeated in the rain? Had he become soaked and chilled, acquiring a life-threatening infection?

It was hard for me to accept that Sal didn't know me. How could he possibly have paged me? He mumbled something about the red liquid and then he began to retch.

An aide placed a tray on a stand between the two stretchers. I lifted up the metal cover and saw the unidentifiable meat of a Bellevue meal.

"Who's supposed to eat this?"

The aide ignored me, and brought trays to the next group of mummified gurney occupants.

Sal had to be transferred to University Hospital immediately. I lifted him off the stretcher and tried to shake him awake. But he was slippery with sweat. He grinned the uncomprehending grin of the very sick and slipped back down through my hands. A nurse stopped me from shaking him again. She grabbed me and pulled me away, full of the strength of working at Bellevue, where lifting heavy patients was part of her routine. But she wasn't the typical Bellevue nurse. She looked to be in her early twenties, most likely a recent nursing-school graduate. She was thin, but her large bones gave her large curves. She wore her blond hair in a bun, and her nurse's uniform was bleached white, strangely unstained for Bellevue. I decided that she must have turned down a job at University Hospital for the challenge of this emergency room.

Without speaking to me, she went to Sal's stretcher and fixed the leaking intravenous line, and the dripping stopped. She dried his face with a towel. Then she went to the other stretcher and looked under the sheet, clearly startled by what she saw there. From the moment she wheeled the other stretcher away, I had a hunch that Sal was about to begin his recovery.

The nurse returned with sponges and a basin, and she began to sponge Sal's face. She worked efficiently, but gently. She was all business, but it was a pleasant business. Sal's breathing slowed to the regular rhythm of sleep. I had never seen this nurse before, but she handled Sal with such tenderness, I was convinced she was one of the nurses who knew him from the wards.

"My name's David," I said, offering her my hand as she was leaving. She squooshed a wet sponge into my palm.

She said, "Sally Wilson."

When Sal was transferred to a regular room later that day, Sally Wilson was no longer his nurse. I kept hoping she would appear, though it would have contradicted the logic of how nurses were assigned. I admired her confidence and her easy manner. Was I spurred on by the possibility that she might have dated Sal?

It was the suddenness of my second meeting with Sally that predicted its success; it lacked the guesswork and innuendoing that might have doomed it. I was on-call that night. Passing the same emergency room alcove, I saw her again. Her shift should have been long over. As before, she was fixing a patient's IV.

"Why are you still here?"

"Doing a double," she said.

"How about a cup of coffee?"

She removed her hair clip and allowed her hair to hang down onto her shoulders, holding the clip in her mouth while she considered me. Then she bunched her hair back up and resecured the clip on top.

"How's Tuesday?" she said. "I finish work at eight."

Since I was the intern on-call, Sal was assigned to be my patient. As far as I knew, no alternative was considered. Who could I appeal to if my feelings for Sal interfered with an intern's routine? But I was determined to help make Sal better. I sat in the doctors' station with the covering resident, poring over Sal's lab work, X rays, and CT scans. They were all normal.

"This is a virus," the covering resident said, a proclamation that did not cheer me.

"Not *the virus.*"

"No. Not necessarily *the virus,*" he said cautiously.

Back when he'd been a medical student, Sal had stuck

himself with a needle after drawing blood from a *virus* patient. He'd been told that the chance of catching *the virus* in this manner was very low, but it was not impossible. At the time, Sal had bragged that the tiny needle covered with deadly blood was almost an allurement. "It's scary. One needle could be enough to finish me," he'd said. Despite his recklessness, he'd scrubbed his hands twenty times with Betadine, then had himself tested for *the virus* antibody. It was easy to mistake Sal's actions for courting death. Actually, he feared death but was an incurable thrill-seeker.

"He's had several negative *virus* antibody tests," I said now to the covering resident, who seemed relieved.

All day and all night, that Thursday, I worried about Kell finding Sal. If Kell knew Sal was a patient, Kell would enter him in the study, exposing him to unknown risks. Whatever the red liquid was, I doubted that it helped the patients. If it were hanging in a bag over Sal's head, I would anticipate a terrible outcome.

But Kell wasn't around the rest of Thursday, and I completed my on-call without incident. Knowing Sal's whereabouts freed me to concentrate on my work. I admitted three new patients besides Sal, two with pneumonia and one with *the virus*. I worked well with the covering resident. I could sense his growing trust in me as I carried out his orders without delay.

Friday morning, Goldman returned. He immediately took charge of Sal's case, showing no sign of his prior animosity. I concluded that Delia must have rejected him. Perhaps Goldman now identified with Sal and feared the same outcome for himself. Whatever the reason, it seemed to me that in caring for Sal, Goldman changed. He was still just as authoritarian, but now he appeared softer, kinder. From Friday on, Goldman drew all Sal's blood tests and prescribed all his medications. He talked about Sal's case for hours, refusing to round or discuss any other patients. I begged Goldman to transfer Sal to University Hospital, but Goldman refused, insisting on treating Sal himself, which meant keeping him at Bellevue. At the same time, Goldman called in thin-boned academics from University Hospital to consult. Sal was getting the VIP treatment all around. X-ray machines showed up in Sal's room before anyone had ordered them, rather than a week late, which was the Bellevue norm. A GONE FISHING sign was posted on the housekeeping office door, but Sal's sheets were changed three times by Friday afternoon.

Sal was alone in a four-bedded room. He had an excellent view of the river, and by late Friday, his eyes were open and he was gazing across at University Hospital.

Friday evening, Sal recovered enough to speak. For the moment he seemed to have forgotten his distrust, and he confided to me that he was cursed. His illness might have the appearance of an infection, but it was really the witch from Catskill spinning her voodoo magic. He said he never should have challenged her.

When I mentioned Sal's belief to Goldman, he scoffed at it. "I wish that's all it was. We could treat him with some special tea, light some incense, and chant around the bedside."

Sal begged me to bring him any doctor but Goldman. Yet when Goldman came to examine him, Sal didn't resist. Sal knew, as I did, that for all Goldman's malice, he was still one of the best doctors in the hospital. And when Goldman left the room, Sal said it wasn't the same malignant Goldman. "He's changed," Sal said.

Goldman was treating Sal with a University antibiotic the Bellevue nurses claimed didn't exist. The Bellevue pharmacy didn't have it, and it wasn't listed in the *Physicians' Desk Reference.* Whatever type of antibiotic it was, it seemed to be working. Goldman said he still didn't know what illness Sal was suffering from, but he had to treat Sal with something. All of Sal's X rays continued to come back negative, and his blood tests were all normal.

There was still no sign of Kell. Sal's chart was missing from the rack. I worried that it would end up in Kell's hands. Friday night, I was post-call, but I didn't go home. I napped in the chair beside Sal's bed. Every time I woke up, I checked the intravenous bag to make sure it hadn't been infiltrated with the red study fluid. I kept the light on in the room so I could tell if the color of the intravenous liquid changed.

The ward nurses visited Sal frequently, bringing him food that Goldman didn't allow him to eat. I ate it instead; spiced chicken, dumplings, two different rice dishes, and three different kinds of cake.

By Saturday, Sal was responding more and more to his surroundings. He eyed me uneasily, as if I were a stranger, or worse, an enemy. When he motioned for me to come closer, I hoped he was shaking the paranoia of his illness. But he whispered in my ear, "Where's Delia?"

He wanted me to bring Delia to him so he could lie with her in the curtainless bed. "I don't know where she is," I said, but Sal didn't seem to believe me. I didn't tell him what I really thought, that Delia wasn't coming to see him, that this time she'd passed him over for good.

Sal's sweats, fevers, and even his weakness had begun to abate. His pale skin and cloudy conjunctiva were changing to a ruddy face and clear eyes. Sunday, he sat up in bed, and he began to eat solid food. When he spoke to me, his voice was strong, though still raspy with the sputum of his illness. Every few minutes he stared at the door, but Delia did not appear there.

"I think you should go to University Hospital, Sal."

"And leave the hospital of last resort? My family has a tradition. I'm the third Vertino to be sick here as an intern."

"Bellevue is not what it was. These days it's all on the backs of the interns and residents and a few devoted nurses."

"That's the way it's always been."

"I bet your grandfather didn't spend all night with patients he couldn't save."

"You're right. In his day they didn't have respirators or monitors."

"What did they do when a patient stopped breathing?"

"What do you think they did? The patient died."

I sighed. "You're making fun of me."

"No. I'm serious. I've begun to appreciate Bellevue. I never meant to come back here, Levy. I thought I could go to the clinic. But I couldn't face Pops. Now I'd like to return to work. I used to hate these derelict patients. I couldn't wait to stick them with needles when they tortured me with their problems. Now I'm ready to help them."

"Sal, I went up there looking for you. Giuseppe showed me your letter."

Sal peered at me with renewed distrust. He left the bed and walked with surprisingly strong steps to the window. When he continued speaking, he didn't seem to notice me, as if I were no longer in the room and he was talking to himself.

"When Delia left, I panicked. It was raining, but I went out to the woods. I got lost . . . I remember making it back out to my car somehow and driving toward the city. I don't know what happened after that . . . I remember pacing the streets behind Bellevue. Someone must have found me and brought me in. I should have waited at Delia's house. She deserves my patience. She's all I've got."

I joined Sal by the window, gazing at the thin lines of clouds that went across Sunday's sky like narrow roads.

"Sal, she'll do it to you again. If you ever do manage to get her back, she'll destroy you. Don't you see how dangerous she is? First it's your career, then it's your health. As soon as you start to feel something for her, she triangles you with someone else."

Sal glared at me, and I braced for his scornful reply. "She's given Goldman up," he said angrily. "And you of all people shouldn't talk about standing up to Goldman. The guy owns you."

"Maybe so. But he's become a lot nicer. He's helping you, and I'm happy for that. You're right, Delia seems to be through with him. Maybe he hates her almost as much as you should."

"Get out of here!"

"Sal! She isn't coming back."

"She'll be here."

He began to cough, a deep retching that took away his breath. He was showering infective droplets all over the room. I went out into the hallway, out of range. His tendency to put me down and his potential to infect me were enough to keep me away for a while.

Down the hall by our doctor's station, Delia was talking with Dr. Kell. Their backs were to me; I couldn't see their faces or easily understand what they were saying. Kell spoke quietly, but Delia's shrill voice carried down the hall. In between Sal's coughs I could hear Delia's words—"*University Hospital . . . virus . . . he has to go . . .*"

Monday I was on call again, and I was assigned a new admission just as I was walking into the hospital. I didn't make it to Sal's room until almost eight. When I arrived, he told me that he'd just been visited by Dr. Kell. There was still no sign of the red liquid, but Sal was visibly upset from the visit.

"He was trying to psychoanalyze me. Said I have low self-esteem, which I compensate for with carelessness and then aggression. When I got upset at this, he told me I'm too sensitive."

"It's like quicksand."

"He said I have an ideal self that is much more successful than my true self. If the two of them come together . . ."

"An explosion?"

Sal laughed staccato chortles of his familiar laughter. I was relieved. By mocking Kell, perhaps we could counteract his taunts. And Sal was returning to health. His choice of clothes reassured me. He'd removed the Bellevue gown and was wearing jeans and one of his favorite flannel shirts. His sneakers were back on his feet, laces untied, without socks.

"Forget Kell, Sal. I spoke to The Boss. The Boss says you can come back to work."

For once Sal really looked at me, registering my presence. We had been friends for a long time. I sat in the chair by his bed, and he patted my shoulder, feeling the cotton material of my lab coat between his fingers. Reaching the Bellevue emblem, he stopped, considering it.

"Delia hasn't been here," he said. "She must think I have *the virus.*"

"What about *the virus,* Sal?" I said softly.

Sal stood straight up, thrusting out his chin.

"I don't have *the virus,* David. I'm just in love."

* * *

As I approached Sal's room an hour later, I encountered Delia, just as she was about to enter. I blocked her, inserting myself in front of the doorway.

"Leave him alone," I insisted.

"I love him," she said simply, as though she could pretend she hadn't mistreated him. My interference didn't deter her. She didn't even say excuse me. She pushed me, and I fell a step backward. She was surprisingly strong. We struggled. Her muscles were as hard as an athlete's. She almost forced me out of the way, but I managed to pressure her back out into the hall. Sal must have been sleeping, because he remained quiet the whole time.

"Asshole!" she said.

"How many times are you going to reject him? Leave him in peace."

"It's not your business. Find your own girlfriend."

"You're not his girlfriend. You go from one to the other. You're nobody's girlfriend."

"I care about him. I love him."

"And how many others?"

"You think I'm a slut?"

"I think you're selfish. You want a challenge. You punish Sal, see how much he can take, and if he survives, you're interested again—for a while."

"You're full of theories," she said angrily. "Why don't you try living."

Sal came out into the hall. Standing, he seemed very weak, and he leaned against the wall for support.

"Leave her alone, Levy," he growled in a low voice.

Delia went to him and helped him back into the room.

When I passed the room an hour later, Sal and Delia were standing by the window. Seeing them there, I lost all hope that he would continue to recover. I didn't go in; there was nothing I could do to stop them. If I hadn't known their history together I would never have been able to predict tragedy from the way she held him with one hand and caressed his neck with the other. I was convinced she would grow bored when she had him all the way back. When he grew weaker again, she would leave him again, no longer caring how he survived.

7

My date with Sally Wilson was planned for eight o'clock Tuesday night. I hadn't spoken to her since Thursday for fear she would cancel. I hoped to see her beforehand, if she visited Sal. But I didn't encounter her in Sal's room, and I worried that our date, if it occurred at all, would seem unnatural. Too much time had passed between encounters. Full of apprehension, nevertheless I planned to meet her in the ER after her shift was over and go from there to a local coffee shop.

By six o'clock Tuesday, all the IVs I'd inserted in the morning had fallen out of the patients' veins. The supply bins had run out of supplies, and most of my patients had left the floor to undergo tests I'd ordered days before. Only the two housekeepers remained, and they demanded immediate attention. When I came to their room they insisted I fix their broken television set.

The more I anticipated leaving, the longer it seemed to take me to accomplish my assignments. The vital-signs sheet listed record highs for blood pressure and temperature. I was post-call, moving in slow motion, still by 7:30 I was almost certain that none of my patients would die overnight. Even the most sadistic resident would probably have agreed that every X ray, every blood test, every box on my list waiting to be x-ed off, could wait until the next morning.

I answered Goldman's final page, and for once, he didn't force me to accept a last-minute patient. I signed out my service to the covering intern. At a quarter to eight, I went to the on-call room for a shower, then changed into the clothes I'd brought in a paper bag two days before. Monday's on-call had been brutal; again no sleep, my food ingested while walking, patients clutching their chests and ceaselessly coughing and vomiting while rolling into the hospital on stretcher after stretcher and being assigned to my care. Deprivation enhanced my appreciation of the slightest pleasure. All day I'd been thinking of nothing but the fresh clothes in the paper bag, the shower, and the hot cup of coffee with Sally.

Before leaving the floor, I stopped by Sal's room for the first time in several hours. He wasn't there. What test had

Goldman sent him for without telling me? A moment later, I realized that the gym bag of supplies and clothes I'd brought from Sal's apartment was missing from beside his bed. I grew worried.

I found the obese nurse who was assigned to him napping at the back of the nurses' station. Shaking her awake, I demanded to know where Sal was.

"Haven't seen him," she said, reclosing her eyes.

I searched the halls until I found my covering intern.

"Where's Vertino?"

I grabbed his arm, but he pulled free and ran off down the hall.

"Goddamn you, Levy! You already signed out to me. I'm on my way to a code!"

I returned to the nurses' station. Sal's nurse remained sitting at the back. She ate a piece of chicken as she told me that a code had come and gone in five minutes; one of my housekeepers had choked on a lobster claw; the on-call resident had performed the Heimlich maneuver.

"That's one even you could have saved, Dr. Levy."

"Where's Vertino!" I barked.

The nurse shrugged, withdrawing another piece of chicken from its cardboard container.

By half past eight, I still hadn't found him. I jumped down fifteen floors of stairs three stairs at a time and ran all the way to the emergency room entrance. Outside, Sally Wilson leaned against the hospital wall. An amputee gestured at her from a filthy, uncovered stretcher no more than two feet away.

"Sally!" I cried, and she saw me and waved. She didn't seem disturbed either by my lateness, or by the vagabond who sought her attention. As I approached them, I saw that the amputee's neck was dark with *bedless* grease. But he was different from the other *bedless*. The heat was stifling, yet a fur coat covered his shoulders. Turning his head to the side, he spat. In profile, his nose appeared crooked. Was he a Rulo look-alike?

Then I saw the identifying wart.

"Rulo! You're at University Hospital. How can you also be here?"

"He says he escaped," Sally Wilson said.

Rulo grinned, eyeing me sideways, as always, trying to gauge my responses. I deliberately didn't look at Sally.

"Dr. Kell meant to test me in his fascist experiment, scanning me on the most invasive of scanners. Science, he called it."

Rulo leaned close to us. He must have been the only patient of the ultramodern University who hadn't had a shower.

"At the last moment—the machines were whirring and I was there in position. A lowly aide was preparing my body when his hand fell across it and I was saved."

Rulo paused, as though he were waiting for me to say something.

"What was it?" Sally said finally.

"The festering swamp, the hideous annoyance."

"Your decubitus? Kell excluded you from his study because of your decubitus?"

"You didn't escape," Sally said. "They sent you back here."

"Back at Bellevue," Rulo said sadly, "I breathe the squalid vapor of the Hades and my fever rises."

"Sally," I said, finally turning to her. "Sal's missing from his room. I don't know what's happened to him."

"The woman plays them all like puppets," Rulo said. "Now a new doctor has her, and while he feasts, your friend starves."

"Sal?" Sally said, not seeming to know whom I meant.

"My friend. The other intern. You were treating him when we met. Don't you know him?"

"You mean Dr. Vertino? I've heard that he's getting better."

"Don't you know him?"

"No. I met him once or twice. He knows how to make the nurses laugh."

Knowing that Sally hadn't dated Sal was an unexpected relief. It was actually *more* flattering to know that she'd chosen to go out with me and she'd hardly noticed him. Perhaps it was possible for me to have my own life, distinct from Sal's tortures and the tortures of Bellevue. Immediately, I started to imagine post-call nights out dancing with Sally, nights spent making love when I was supposed to be sleeping.

"Maybe your friend has gone to University Hospital," Sally said.

"That's what I'm afraid has happened."

"But he'll get much better care there. Maybe the faculty can figure out what's wrong with him."

"Originally, that seemed like a good idea. But Dr. Kell hates Vertino. Now I'm afraid Kell has taken him to University Hospital to study him. Over there, Goldman can't stop it."

Sally looked at me curiously, and I was thankful that she didn't call me paranoid or say I was overworked. Rulo had become uncharacteristically quiet, and now, as he spoke, he once again seemed to be an oracle.

"No, your friend has not crossed the river. He pursues his passion, at great personal risk. Kell seeks him out. Your friend is in danger."

The way Sally was staring at Rulo, I knew it was time for us to leave or our date would be entirely ruined. As we helped him lie back on his stretcher, I felt Sally's strength. I was so anxious to leave that as soon as Rulo was situated, I began to walk off. Happily, Sally decided to come with me, and Rulo stayed where he was.

"You don't know how to save him, Dr. Levy," he called after me.

All the way to the coffee shop, I tried to dismiss Rulo's assertion. Couldn't Sal have crossed to University Hospital without Rulo knowing it? Could Rulo be delirious as a result of Dr. Kell's study? I looked behind me to make sure he wasn't following us. We passed the Mayfield Apartments, the gray, monolithic tower where Sally lived. Sally told me that these apartments were oversized closets provided at a low rent to the staff of University Hospital. Sally believed that University owned housing on this side of the river to entice potential nurses. The University nursing administration would offer a studio to a Bellevue nurse like Sally to try to get her to switch hospitals.

Walking with Sally, I felt less anxious. She talked about her apartment so easily, so soon after meeting me—perhaps this was flirting.

The coffee shop of Sally's choice was really more of a café. We sat at a table that overlooked the street. A GELATO/CAPPUCCINO neon sign flashed red in the window. My anxiety returned. An awkward silence developed between us until the waiter came, and we both ordered cappuccinos.

"Do you know the red liquid?" I asked Sally. The waiter smiled as he was leaving.

"Is it a medicine?"

"It might be a narcotic. What color is morphine?"

"Clear," she said.

"Demerol?"

"Clear."

A good nurse knew many things an intern didn't know. Interns routinely prescribed medications they'd never seen.

"Most solutions are colorless," she lectured. "Vitamins are yellow. Proteins are also yellow, and lipids are white."

"Why is he using a red liquid?"

"Who?"

I didn't answer.

"What about blood?" she suggested.

"No. Blood's not a liquid."

"Not a liquid?"

Sally laughed and relaxed. She flipped the hair back

from her face, and I could see her ears redden with the pleasure of correcting me. The waiter came with our cappuccinos. We drank them. Hers made a thin mustache on her upper lip. Her leg brushed my leg, and after a moment, I brushed her leg back. I felt better again. Soon we were holding hands. Our hands were wet. I thought, *We will be lovers.*

"What if that patient's right?" she said, and I was immediately tense.

"I'm sure Sal's at University Hospital. His stuff is gone from Bellevue."

"Let's go there."

"Let's call there. See if he's on their list of patients."

"We have to go there," she said.

She offered to pay the check, but I said I would pay. I apologized for coming late. She smiled and said she would forgive me. We left the café and walked back toward Bellevue. After the chill of the air-conditioning, the outside air was warm. I wanted to go hear jazz. But tonight's music would be the sputter of the old Toyota engine, the static of its radio straining to receive a station.

At the Bellevue parking lot, Sally kissed me, immediately improving my mood. She waited at the entrance while I went to get the car. Striding up the ramp, I watched her watching me.

Vertino's Alfa was backed into its usual corner spot, covered with weeks of dust. Since he never traveled anywhere without his car, I was even more convinced that he'd been taken, against his will, to University Hospital.

My Toyota was also in its customary place, parked front-end-in alongside a concrete pole. After several tries, the Toyota finally started, and I drove it rattling down the ramp to Sally. Smiling again, she yanked on the rusty handle until the door opened. As soon as she was inside, I took off, turning onto the street, trying to impress her with the Toyota's version of acceleration. But the vapor locks took hold, and the car lurched and bucked.

We traveled north on the highway, taking the bridge at Fifty-ninth Street, crossing the dark river and connecting to a parallel highway on the other side. The potholes disappeared, and the car no longer rattled. I followed the H sign, exiting onto a road paved with sparkling blacktop. After another half a mile we came to a large parking lot. I parked the car beneath a STAFF sign and looked up at a maze of glass buildings.

"Which is University Hospital?"

"Wait here," Sally said. "They won't let you in. It's after ten."

"But I'm staff."

"Interns are considered Bellevue staff."

"What about you?"

We left the car, and I followed Sally through the parking lot. She walked quickly. All of a sudden she seemed caught up in the charisma of the place. She no longer responded to me.

"Wait," I said. "Which building is University Hospital?"

We reached the entrance to emergency just as an ambulance with blaring sirens and flashing lights pulled up. The ambulance was beautiful. It was large and clean and shining. Painted on the side in gold letters was the word UNIVERSITY. Two attendants jumped out of the back and opened the rear doors. They removed a collapsible gurney and snapped it open.

Sally walked on. I stood near the ambulance as the paramedics carried out the patient. When I moved closer, the paramedics glared at me. It was clear that they didn't expect or want my help.

Did I know him? His hair was curly, and the skin of his face was creased with adhesive tape, making him look as if he were smiling. A breathing tube protruded from his neck.

The paramedics didn't move him into the hospital right away. One paramedic felt the groin for a pulse while the other one attached an Ambu Bag to the tube in the neck and breathed him. Despite their efforts, his face turned gray. All at once they did move him; one paramedic forcing air into the lungs, the other pumping on the chest as they raced him in.

I followed them as far as the glass doors of the emergency entrance. A small clerk with large whiskers and a mole in the center of his forehead stopped me.

"Let me see your badge," he said.

"I don't have it here. But you have to let me in. I'm an intern. I'm with the patient."

"You're not with the patient. You're from Bellevue."

"You expect me to go all the way around to the main entrance?"

"They won't let you in there either. It's past visiting hours."

"This is fucking ridiculous," I said.

"You want to be reported for using inappropriate language?"

"Reported to whom? In order to report me, first you have to accept that I work here."

"You don't have identification. You don't work here."

"You let my friend through."

"Sally Wilson? They've offered her a nursing position."

"You know her?!"

"Of course, Dr. Levy," he said, winking.

"How do you know me?"

The clerk didn't answer. Instead, he left his post and stepped on the mat of plush red carpeting before the spotless glass doors. Instantly, the doors whirred open and the clerk passed through. I tried to follow him, but the doors smacked closed in my face. I stomped on the carpeted mat, but University Hospital would not reopen.

8

University Hospital was not an ordinary institution. Built at a time of great opulence and expanse in medicine, it survived into the era of cutbacks and capitation, where medical care was parceled out patient by patient like wartime sugar. The University, meanwhile, continued to amass millions of dollars in research grants and endowments from billionaires. No doubt some of this funding was utilized to keep the regulatory commissions looking to the other side of the river, while University Hospital continued catering to its favorite patients and the poor man and the workingman were taken by ambulance to Bellevue. Almost every year an ordinance was presented to the city council, proposing improved access for the public to University facilities. Almost every year this ordinance was championed in the local newspapers only to be voted down in council session or tabled to the following year. The end result was that Bellevue, rather than University Hospital, came to be under greater and greater scrutiny. Quality-control people worked over every Bellevue ward, penalizing the institution for the perpetual internment of the biters and the Larcombes. Official proclamations banning *the bedless* from hospital grounds were drawn up in legal language and posted everywhere. For a time following each proclamation, *the bedless* relocated. But the good-hearted members of the staff continued to leave stretchers by the river, and slowly, each time they were banned, *the bedless* returned.

Bellevue didn't have money; intravenous and blood-drawing equipment were scarce. The operating room closed down periodically until it reaccrued enough sterile equipment to operate. Interns had to guess which medications the pharmacy was stocking, and patients were turned away. In mid-July of my internship, the pharmacy ran out of most of its medications and told all the patients to return in a week.

The virus was rampant, but there was no foreseeable cure, and Bellevue was overwhelmed with *virus* patients. Each one harbored ten different infections or tumors that had yet to be diagnosed. And treating their known problems was all consuming. If I slept fifteen minutes while on call, I'd think, *I've slept, I've slept,* and I'd try to assume some sort of mental order. By mid-morning I'd be disoriented. By the post-call afternoon I'd hit the mental wall; a fifteen-minute chore took me an hour to perform. I'd become paranoid that those who worked shifts could tell I was afflicted. The nurses would ask me, "Are you on call, are you post-call?" How could I fool them? Long after dark I'd go stumbling home, and I would feel, as many interns have described the sensation, as if I'd been released from prison. Once home, I'd talk on the telephone to anyone I could reach, cherishing my few free hours, staving off sleep until it overcame me. The following morning I'd awaken stiff as old luggage, on the floor, or in my bed, not remembering how I'd gotten there.

I'd return again to Bellevue, though Bellevue always seemed changed in the few hours I'd spent away from it. I'd pass through the emergency room on my way back upstairs. In the predawn hours, at the heart of the emergency room, the Crash Room would be still, its floors shining from a late-night mopping. Housekeeping assigned its only regular working detail to the pride of Bellevue. Victims of sudden heart attacks, stabbings, gunshots, and motor vehicle accidents were brought here. Surgical saws and needles sparkled on the shelves and counters. The industrial-tile floors had large drains. Every surgical need I could think of was mounted to the walls, and oversized centrifuges on the counters could spin down blood in seconds. Despite its terrible deficiencies as a hospital, surprisingly, as a place to treat injury, sudden heart attack, or stroke, Bellevue was top-notch. In the predawn hours, the Crash Room would often be quiet and clean, ready for its next accident victim.

* * *

The Toyota wouldn't start. A vapor lock had overcome the engine. The starter turned over without ignition, weakening the battery until there wasn't a sound when I turned the key. The vapor lock was mushrooming into something more serious.

It was eleven o'clock, and I was alone in the parking lot. The sky was dark, clear but without a moon. The lights in the parking lot shut off automatically, obeying a hidden timer. The glass walls of University Hospital shimmered, lit from within by powerful lamps. Which was the main hospital building? From across the river it seemed like a single building, but up close, University Hospital was a complex of structures twenty to thirty stories tall without an apparent center. Sally Wilson had entered this maze at ten. An hour later, she still hadn't returned.

At half past eleven, the night crew would begin to arrive. Midnight was the change of shift. By half past twelve, the last of the evening staff would leave the hospital for home.

There was a faint tap at the car window. It was Sally. She looked exhausted.

"He's not here," she said.

"I didn't know if you were coming back."

"The computers are down, so I had to check every ward myself. Do you know how many wards there are?"

I got out of the car as Sally was about to get in.

"Are you sure he's not here?"

"Positive. Your crazy patient was right. There's nothing more we can do. Let's go."

"You drive," I said. She seemed puzzled, but followed my instruction as soon as I told her that the car wouldn't start. She put the car in neutral, and I pushed the Toyota past a manicured lawn. A display of orange and red tropical flowers was visible in the dark. Laughing, Sally steered wildly down a small hill, and when the car picked up speed, I yelled for her to put it in gear and then let out the clutch. The Toyota lurched, coughed, then sputtered into action. Sally turned on the headlights, stepped on the gas pedal, and the car pulled away from me. She opened the passenger-side door, and I ran as fast as I could run, jumped in, and off we sped, accelerating to avoid a stall.

Driving back, we didn't discuss Sal. Silence ruled in the Toyota. Our fruitless search had upset our thin alliance—the best a first date could hope for. Sally drove slowly and carefully. When she stopped the car at Mayfield Apartments, I told her I didn't want her to leave without first hearing how grateful I was for her help. This was a good thing to say. She relaxed, hugging me and then kissing me, darting her tongue onto mine for a brief second. I could hardly wait for our next date.

"Don't worry," she said. "We'll find him. He's probably back at Bellevue already."

She walked away, slumped over from fatigue. But when she reached the doorman, she turned, smiling as I drove away, waving as I puttered slowly out of her sight.

My adrenal glands finally lost their battle with lack of

sleep, and my eyes began to close. Somehow I drove the five blocks to my apartment. I parked out front by a broken meter. I would return the Toyota to Bellevue in the morning—before they fixed the meter.

By six the next morning, I'd forgotten about the car. I awoke in my clothes, lying on the bedroom floor, my head on the carpet, my arms wrapped around the bottom of my bed. A shower and fresh clothes didn't refresh me. A little sleep made me aware of a greater fatigue. I returned stiff leggedly to the hospital.

I pushed myself through pre-rounds, making new lists on top of old lists. I couldn't remember which boxes to x off, and which to leave blank because the tests were still pending. So I ordered X rays and performed EKGs on everyone. I examined chests, hearts. When I came to the two housekeepers, they both insisted on having rectal exams, though they'd declined this humiliating procedure previously. Both men were strangely cooperative—was the rectal another angle they could exploit for extended benefits or prolonged length of stay?

Sal wasn't back in his hospital room. I phoned his apartment repeatedly, but there was no answer.

Larcombe was alone in his room. He didn't move when I examined him. I could hear the air whistling in and out through his breathing tube, so I knew he was alive. The sheet rope lay in a heap by his bed. If a housekeeper had finally untied it from the railing, it would be several more days before another housekeeper was authorized to remove it from the room.

At 8 A.M. I went to the chart rack, but Goldman remained in the doctors' station, leaning against the wall glass with his eyes closed.

"Are we going to round?"

"Sure," he said. He didn't open his eyes.

I tapped him on the shoulder. Finally, he looked at me. I showed him my clipboard with the new patient list, and he nodded, closing his eyes again. He didn't have his cigarettes or his soda container.

"Where's Vertino?" he asked me.

"Officially, he's still here."

"But he's not here. Dr. Kell has seen to that."

"And he's not at University Hospital either."

Goldman opened his eyes and regarded me carefully. "That's right," he agreed. "So where is he?"

A worried expression had taken the place of the sadistic glint that had haunted me from the first day of internship. Goldman was overcome by a sudden choking cough. His eyes watered, and he waited for several seconds before continuing. I had a feeling that the next subject was Dr. Kell.

"Last night," he said, "Kell signed Sal out of this hospital—against medical advice."

"Where could Sal go in his condition?"

"Who knows."

"But, officially, Sal's still at Bellevue?"

"That's right."

Goldman's breathing was slow, and I was calmed by his large, suffering presence. He'd reached out with his substantial skills as a physician to save Sal. Kell's games outraged even Goldman. Goldman was for the patient.

Suddenly I remembered that I'd left the Toyota parked illegally in front of my apartment. I excused myself from rounds. Goldman hardly seemed to notice.

Running home, I arrived at my apartment just as the tow truck turned the corner. I jumped into the Toyota and it started right up. I drove back to Bellevue without a single stall. In the parking lot for the first time in several hours, I discovered that Sal's space was empty. I drove through the lot, but the Alfa was gone.

I decided not to tell Goldman that Sal had driven away in his car. Obviously, Goldman was concerned: He'd been beaten down to an approachable humility by Delia; he'd even helped Sal to get better, but he still wasn't my confidant.

Dr. Kell's Bellevue secretary said he was across the river, tending to his private patients. Dr. Kell's University secretary insisted he was at Bellevue. I telephoned The Boss's secretary, who couldn't seem to believe that an intern was calling The Boss. She took the message, but I knew The Boss would never get it.

Delia stood with Bruce and Michael outside by the coffee truck. Bruce was holding a cup of coffee, and as I watched, Delia snatched the cup from his hand and drank from it. She smacked Michael on the thigh, and he cavorted, dancing backward. The male students' shirts were open at the collar, and their ties were missing. It was very hot for this early in the morning, and Bruce and Michael sweated abundantly, though they didn't seem to care. Their hair was unruly, and they both needed a shave. They laughed, performing for Delia. I'd heard that Bruce and Michael had experienced plummeting grades since being assigned to their new team. They would probably have to repeat their entire medical rotation.

When I tried to pass them to get to Delia, they blocked my way with their shoulders.

"What's happening to Sal Vertino?" I shouted through them.

She appeared unaffected by the heat. She was hardly sweating. She motioned the bodyguards aside and strode up to me. She surveyed me without emotion.

"I have no idea where your friend is," she said, and she dismissed me with a cold glance.

9

The day was hot; the sky and the river were both bluer than a chronic lunger's face. Presently, the man inside the coffee truck would come out and open the metal doors. The truck served us stale coffee all night, but in the early morning it shut down, reopening now in the late morning with doughnuts and fresh coffee.

Delia hung on Bruce's and Michael's shoulders, rubbing their sweaty necks. Bruce and Michael giggled like adolescents. Soon they would be laughing at the most somber of bedsides. If they were perceived as insolent, a threat to the hierarchy, then other medical students would be assigned to observe them, and their careers would be in jeopardy.

Delia spun her web in a highly visible environment where even a medical student's moves could affect a patient's life. So much was expected of a student so quickly that a week goofing off was enough to derail the most capable. For an intern like Sal, there was even less margin for error. Delia knew this. I suspected it was part of what enticed her. The more a man was willing to sacrifice, the more important she must have felt. Surely she kept her own grades up, coolly preparing for her next exam while her latest conquest obsessed, trying to guess what she was thinking.

Delia didn't have the same effect on me, though I feared her. I was intimidated by her power to make a man feel special and then her need to take it away. Even as my anger for Sal grew, I didn't challenge her. Sal had always seemed oblivious to her maneuvering and had gone on acting fearless.

If Sal were back at her house, would she admit it?

The three medical students approached the coffee truck, looking curiously at the closed doors.

"Today's a holiday," Bruce said suddenly.

"No it isn't," I said. Bruce ignored me. In fact, all three ignored me. I continued to stand near them, shifting uneasily, transferring my weight from one leg to the other. Where was Sal? Would observing Delia provide me with a clue? I felt so demeaned. Bruce and Michael's disregard went beyond their need to impress Delia. Since I was no longer part of a teaching service, few respected me. Medical students were locked into the pecking order. They were used to receiving and transferring abuse. They were bound to ridicule me now that I lacked the slightest authority. Nurses tended not to respect me either, no matter how hard I worked. Only the residents (including Goldman) seemed to recognize my growing efficiency, and for this I was grateful.

Bruce tapped lightly on the window of the coffee truck, but the man inside still didn't come out, and the coffee truck suddenly drove off.

"Hey," Michael yelled. He ran after it, catching up and pounding on the flimsy metal doors. "Open up!"

The coffee truck continued going, accelerating away from the students.

Giggling, arm in arm, the three went back inside the hospital, without even a glance at me. I didn't follow them. Whatever Delia was hiding, I wouldn't find it out by stalking.

I stayed outside for several minutes, feeling beaten. When I finally went inside, overcoming the emergency entrance doors after several tries, I discovered a large housekeeping memo pasted to the wall. Bruce was right. Today was a holiday unique to Bellevue, honoring Gerald Johnson and Samuel Jefferson, founders of the housekeeping union. According to the memo, medical business was to go on as usual, but the concessions were closed—the florist, the barber shop, the card store that dispensed its cards to patients in exchange for aluminum cans. The clerks had the day off, and all the housekeepers were invited to the room of my two housekeeper patients for a catered affair. The memo mentioned that the mayor of the city and all his assistants were also invited.

The skeletal staff during a Bellevue holiday was bound to be even less effective than usual. Nurses' notes would be pure fiction. Patients with fevers, sweats, and mental changes would be reported as "within normal limits" five minutes before being rushed to intensive care. A patient about to have a massive heart attack would be listed as sleeping if the housekeepers had invited the patient's nurse to their party.

But this wasn't a holiday for interns or residents. When I returned upstairs to the medical ward I discovered that all four medical teams were still at full strength.

Throughout the day, all four doctors' stations remained busy. Even on the pathetic nonteaching service the work tripled because the nurses were too busy with the party to assist me. Goldman, despite his depressed state, ate several pounds of party food and then fell asleep on his couch in the on-call rooms. Paper plates loaded with seafood and pasta were brought from the housekeepers' room and circulated from nurse to nurse. I struggled to complete my work but fell rapidly behind. I intended to investigate Sal's disappearance further, but I was kept from following through the entire day by continual patient complaints.

The party ended abruptly when The Biter left a gift of his excrement outside the party door. Apparently The Biter was mad because the housekeeper patients had accused him of stealing their *Times,* which was delivered to their room every morning by special messenger. This morning the housekeepers had attached a string to the newspaper, but when they'd followed the string, it had led them to Larcombe.

The excrement stayed outside the door for several hours, with no housekeepers officially on duty to remove it, because of the holiday. I doubted the housekeepers would ever repay The Biter for his gift; they were too afraid of what he might do for an encore.

By the middle of the afternoon, I was very hungry, but by the time I got to the housekeepers' room the excrement was there and all the party food had been consumed. The red light on the candy bar machine by the elevator was flashing EXACT CHANGE ONLY, and I didn't have any change. All interns had tickets that could be exchanged in the cafeteria for unlimited food. But the acrid smell of fish batter that had been reused too many times permeated the cafeteria, the meat was unidentifiable, and the coffee smelled like elementary school hot chocolate. Most doctors ate in the Greek coffee shop on the ground floor. Goldman took all his meals there, but as an intern I only had time for coffee and a sandwich to go. The countermen were artists of the sandwich for whom rye bread was *whiskey;* lettuce, tomato, and cheese were a *full house,* and cream cheese was *c.c.* An order for a tuna sandwich with lettuce, cheese, and tomato on toasted rye bread was translated into counterese and shouted by the counterman to the cook as "*Tuna full house whiskey down.*"

I took the elevator down to the ground floor. As I approached the coffee shop, a crowd of reporters and photographers bustled past me, probably following the mayor to the housekeepers' room, where he was about to find a surprise.

The coffee shop was almost empty. The chalkboard listed sirloin steak as the housekeeper special of the day. In the glass cabinet under the counter there were several cakes in the shape of mops.

I took a seat at the counter, but then someone called out, "Let me buy you a cup of coffee." I looked up. Delia Meducci was sitting in a small booth in the corner—alone.

"Let me buy you a cup of coffee," she repeated. Could she be talking to me? I put a finger to my chest and mouthed "Me?" She smiled, nodding.

I went to her booth and sat across from her, still incredulous at the invitation. She moved forward until her breasts were resting on the table. We both wore green scrub shirts, but her V neck was deeper, and I had an unprecedented view through the cloth window. The tops of her breasts looked like pictures of breasts, suspended out at ninety degrees by Cooper's ligaments. She leaned even closer, and her elbows were almost touching my elbows. I was suspicious of her sudden interest. I decided to wait before bringing up the subject of Sal.

The waiter stood by the table and cleared his throat. I ordered coffee and a toasted blueberry muffin.

"Bleeeewbeeeeerrrry all the way down," the waiter bellowed across the room to the cook.

"Just coffee for me," Delia said.

A moment later the waiter returned and slammed down our coffees.

"Poor Sal. I tried to help him," Delia said.

"His car is gone. You must know where he is."

"His car is gone?"

I didn't accept her façade, but I couldn't call her a liar and expect to find out anything. Her feigned sympathy was nauseating.

"I didn't want to hurt him," she said. "But he was so dependent. Clinging to me."

"What about Dr. Kell?"

Delia blushed. She picked up my stethoscope from the table and held it by an earpiece, swinging the weighted bell back and forth. Then she ran her hand along the black length. I tried to take it from her, but she wouldn't let go of it. I thought, *Give it to me. It's only a stethoscope.*

"Dr. Kell?" she said.

I was going to mention Sal's letter, but I decided it wasn't a good idea to give Delia new information to work with. Also, the more I confronted her, the less likely she would be to tell me the truth about Kell.

She looked down at the table, using my stethoscope to knock away the crumbs that remained from the previous customer. After a few long moments, the waiter brought my blueberry muffin.

"You must have heard from Sal," I said. "Did you see his car? What if something's happened?"

She looked up at me, studying my face. "I'm worried about him too. He's not at my house."

I was startled when she mentioned her house. She seemed to know that I had been there. Also, I was sure she'd stopped herself from completing the sentence. The next word was *anymore. "He's not at my house anymore."*

My beeper wailed, startling me again. I rose from the table, slurping a last sip of coffee as I grabbed my stethoscope back from her and flung it around my neck. The waiter looked at me curiously.

"Wrap it up to go," I told him.

Delia stood also.

"What do you want me to do?"

"Tell me what Kell has to do with this mess."

She wouldn't look at me. "I don't know," she said.

"Is Sal in Kell's study?"

"I don't know."

If only she'd agreed that things had gone too far, I might have been able to think of her in more human terms.

I put a $5 bill on the table and left the coffee shop. She followed me out into the hall. But I lost sight of her in another sudden crowd of dignitaries and flashbulb-popping photographers. By the time I found a wall phone to answer my page, Delia was gone.

"Outside call," the page operator said.

The voice was muffled, almost unrecognizable.

"They're coming to kill me. If I stay here, I'll die. If I move, I'll die."

"Where are you!?"

"I'm so afraid. What can I do?"

"Stay right where you are. I'll come get you."

"You can do that?"

"Of course I can."

"Aren't you working? Don't you have to work?"

"Where are you, Sal?!"

"Oh God, I'm so afraid."

The mechanical termination voice interrrupted, asking Sal for more change. I knew I had to keep him on the phone while I arranged to get him help. But a moment later there was static, followed by the dial tone.

I called the page operator back on STAT page and demanded to be reconnected.

"Connected to where?"

"Don't you know where these calls are coming from?"

"Dr. Levy, are you joking?"

I hung up and dialed Sal's apartment, but of course there was no answer. Next I called the Bellevue security office, but an answering machine announced that security was closed for the holiday. I stood by the phone, stamping my feet in frustration. A nurse who worked with Sally Wilson tapped me on the shoulder. Her smile and warm greeting reassured me that Sally probably wanted me to call her again. But this was the worst possible time to think of it. I tried to walk away, but the nurse reminded me that a rule-out-*the-virus* patient I'd admitted during my on-call two days before was still down in the ER. Because of the holiday, her bed still wasn't ready. The nurse said the patient was spiking a temperature and looking poorly. *What about Sal?* I almost roared at her. Sal was full of paranoid delusions. He was in terrible trouble. I had to find him before something happened to him. But I had no idea where he was.

I forced myself to follow the nurse to the patient's alcove in the ER.

It was hot in the alcove. The patient, a young woman with bitemporal wasting, lay on a stretcher that was soaked through with her sweat. She was wrapped tightly in a blanket. She rolled on her stretcher and moaned. The nurse must have told her my full name, because she repeated it over and over.

"David Levy."

"Here I am."

A shadow passed over the alcove and the temperature dropped, but when I looked behind me there was no one there. I had the momentary sensation of an unnatural presence.

The post beside the patient's stretcher was wet. Without thinking, I touched the post with my ungloved finger. As an intern, I knew the feel of blood instantly.

I washed my hands twenty times with Betadine at the closest sink.

When I returned to the patient I realized how wasted-looking she was. Her ears had thinned to the thickness of paper, and her nose and chin had been reduced to their essential cartilage and bone. She was probably about thirty years old, but she looked ten years older.

"I've been expecting David Levy," she said. "Have you seen him?"

"I am Dr. Levy!"

"Where is David Levy? He's supposed to come."

I concluded that either she couldn't hear me, or else she

was completely delirious from infection. She opened her mouth, revealing the red and white patches of yeast, emblems of immunocompromise. She shivered, closing her eyes. She breathed more quickly—shallow breaths. I thought, *She needs the respirator.*

I paged Goldman and begged him to come down. He reluctantly agreed, though he still sounded depressed and half asleep. While I was waiting for him, I went outside. To this day, I don't know what happened to the patient in the alcove. I think of her every time I test negative for *the virus*. But in the confusion and hysteria of everything that was about to happen, this patient was lost. I don't know if she was admitted to the hospital and reassigned to another intern. Perhaps she left the hospital against medical advice, crawling out the door while I was occupied with the most devastating event of my life. It was weeks before I remembered her, and then when I searched the lists of patients alive and dead, I couldn't find her name. I still remember, though, her final words as I was leaving her: "Where is David Levy?" she asked. "Bring him here!"

The coffee truck was back, despite the holiday. I waited on the short line and ordered a large cup of coffee. The weather actually seemed cooler than in the morning. It was a beautiful afternoon. I stood near the hospital and watched the highway.

Where was Sal? Where had he called me from?

Several cars zoomed past, traveling well beyond the speed limit. The small tree between the road and the river seemed almost tropical; it was blooming—an angular red flower as though someone were watering it secretly with liquid from Dr. Kell's study. Under the highway, a *bedless* lay directly on the concrete, cushioned only by his emaciated buttocks. He peeled away his clothes, layer by brown layer. Over his head, the cars roared. The river coursed at his feet. Had an off-duty clerk removed his stretcher?

I drank my coffee slowly. I was hoping that Delia would show up while I was out here. If I told her about Sal's desperate phone call, she would become even more frightened. She really had no choice. She had to help me find him.

As I was finishing my coffee, Rulo wheeled up. Sunlight reflected off the metal arms and spokes of his wheelchair.

"Victor. I'm looking for Delia Meducci, the medical student. Have you seen her?"

Rulo wheeled closer, seeming glad for my attention.

"She wears clothes like yours. She calls you friend. 'A cup of coffee?' she asks, eliciting your compassion. Dr. Levy, beware her metamorphosis. Her painful-to-the-touch armor resecretes. She has rejected your friend. Whenever her energy ebbs, she assumes a guise and approaches another victim."

"Rulo, is Vertino in great danger?"

"Am I the all-knowing? The all-seeing?"

"Yesterday you told me he wasn't at University Hospital, and you were right. Is Kell pursuing him?"

Rulo squinted at me, and I suddenly saw him as a derelict in someone else's clothes. He wasn't clairvoyant. He was a con artist, or worse.

"Do you confront your enemy? Or do you confront me instead, at the height of my misery, paralyzed as I am by the goddamn sleeplessness?"

"Is it Kell?"

Rulo smiled. "You seek my help, but do you bring me even a single pill? Perhaps a sandwich to ease my hunger? You approach me at the most ungodly hour. Look at the hour; it is no longer within the single digits! You demand explanations. I, who am helpless, you insist I help you. And what are you prepared to offer me in return? Shall we say, unofficially?"

I decided that Rulo didn't know where Sal was. I walked away from him.

"Beware!" Rulo warned. "The angel of death. You've waited too long."

I stamped my feet on the entrance mat, and for once, the emergency room doors screeched open.

"You're too late!" Rulo called after me.

My extra beeper, the beeper for cardiac arrests, sounded a preemptory shriek, but then it was quiet. As I neared my patient's alcove, my name was announced overhead on the loudspeaker. I dropped the empty paper coffee cup onto the floor. A moment later the cardiac arrest beeper wailed for real, and I went from standing still to an all-out sprint.

The code was coming from outside the hospital. These were the ones who never made it. By the time the paramedics brought them in, the elapsed time was too long. We went through our motions, filling their veins with our strongest medicines and shocking them with electricity. We pumped on their chests. This was the ritual. We ran to the codes at our fastest speed. Sometimes we injured ourselves on the way. When we got there, the patients were already dead. And Bellevue, not University, was the city center for these deaths.

Luckily, I was already on the ground floor. An elevator never brought me down fast enough for a cardiac arrest. The elevator regulars refused to give up their control of the elevator.

When I reached the Crash Room, the nurses were getting ready. They were hanging IV bags on to poles, drawing medications into syringes, moving monitors and IV poles into position around a six-foot-long area.

The stretcher came in, with the paramedics surrounding it. One paramedic bagged air into the patient's lungs. Another pumped on his chest. There was a lot of blood. Sometimes, with a bullet wound, there was so much blood that it obscured the part of the body that had been shot. But the paramedics didn't announce that this had been a shooting.

I didn't see Fat Goldman come in, but now he was leaning over the stretcher, barking orders, pumping on the chest himself, wheezing with the effort, his bare arms covered with a mixture of sweat and blood. He called for the breathing tube and a scalpel, and then he slashed a path into the patient's neck, inserting the breathing tube in a way that was supposed to be left to the surgeons. When the stability of the spine was in question, the surgeons bypassed the standard intubation procedure through the mouth and performed an emergency tracheostomy.

The surgeons came into the room, smiling and pointing at the patient's neck. Goldman stepped back, and now the surgeons were in charge. The chief resident surgeon took a position at the head of the stretcher and called out the orders.

"Motor vehicle accident," he announced, which set into motion a set pattern of nurse and doctor responses: the surgical protocol for treating a car-accident victim.

He was smaller than I expected a surgeon to be, but the other surgical residents jumped at the sound of his voice. He was the authority here, the ruler of the Crash Room. No attending surgeon would supervene unless the patient made it to the operating room. The director of the ER had tried to wrest control of the Crash Room away from the surgical residents, but the surgeons had prevailed by providing The Boss a list of deaths resulting from the ineptitude of the ER residents.

One surgeon took over the chest pumping, while another Ambued air through the breathing tube into the lungs. A third surgeon placed large-bore intravenous lines into veins in both the patient's arms, and the nurses ran the fluid in as fast as it could go.

As a medical intern, I couldn't get very close. I stood at the EKG machine and watched its paper run. The heart rhythm was no rhythm, a single uninterrupted flat line along the paper, but when the medical resident next to me shouted this information to the surgeon in charge, he appeared to ignore her.

"Women haters," she whispered to me, but I thought

the surgeons ignored *all* medical residents, with the exception of Fat Goldman.

I looked around the room for Delia, but I didn't see her.

The charged paddles were applied repeatedly to the patient's chest, and he was shocked with electricity, yet the heart rhythm remained asystole, flat line. The crowd of surgeons and nurses surrounding the stretcher blocked my view. The paper left the EKG machine and flowed down onto the floor beside me.

Next they opened the chest, not because it would help the patient, but because they were surgeons. Blood seemed to be coming from everywhere. There was the sound of rib cutters being applied to bone. One of the surgeons reached inside the chest and held the patient's heart in his hands, squeezing it. A heart became strangled as the blood ran out of a body through torn flesh and the tiny arteries that supplied the heart crimped without blood. In the end, the heart betrayed itself, cutting off its own blood supply, bloating up, a wasted balloon. The body's greatest muscle turned to sump, a bag of still blood, as the patient turned gray and edematous, his brain gone, his eyes acquiring that fixed stare.

I still could not see through the crowd.

Then, with a single wave of his arm, the surgeon in charge called the code off, and the crowd backed away, and I was able to see. Only Goldman was left, working over the patient's neck with a needle and a syringe, obscuring the patient's face from me. No one dared to pull Goldman off. No one came forward and asked him to stop. Finally, with his arms flopping like fins to his sweaty sides, Goldman too stepped back.

The flesh was still the color of flesh. It was the color of life. The tube protruding from the neck could have been drawing in breaths. The thick nose and its nostrils could still have been dilating with air. But the arms and the sneakered feet drooped down off the gurney. And the eyes were as still as fish eyes. The empty space, where the head surgeon had been, told the story to those who joined the crowd at the very end. Still flushed with the pride of life, the body appeared warm before the final effects of entropy. Through all the bloody curls of hair and the shards of glass embedded in the face, I could finally see him now, and I could know him.

PART FOUR

PURGATORY

July 16th

10

Still warm, the body had lain under a sheet. In the morning, when the undertaker had come to Giuseppe's clinic, the undertaker had sought some assurance that the man was really dead.

I knew then there was a curse, Sal had said.

In the Crash Room, I repeated to myself over and over, *Sal couldn't be dead. He couldn't really be dead. Could he?*

I shrank from the body, as if I could blot it out, as if I could will Sal back to life Larcombe-style as long as I didn't confirm the physical findings.

"Delia!" I shouted, but there was no response.

I sat against the wall, on the sticky Crash Room floor, for long uncounted minutes as the nurses cleaned the body. Was it becoming cold?

Finally, Fat Goldman came and led me from the Crash Room.

Goldman telephoned the sick-call intern and ordered him to substitute for me. An hour later I was driving the Toyota down a small road somewhere in Westchester. There were so many forks in the road, soon I was lost. The white line faded and disappeared. The road turned to gravel. Was I still in Westchester? The Toyota was low on fuel. The needle fluctuated; the gauge read full with a turn to the left, empty with a turn to the right. The road twisted and doubled back on itself.

Thump, thump, badump. A rear tire was going flat. I stopped.

The spare tire was nestled deep in the trunk like a fetus in its womb. It was slick with old water that must have leaked in through the lid. I yanked the tire free and bounced it on the gravel. It barely bounced.

In my old Toyota, the crowbar was also the lug wrench. I slammed it against the gravel until the rust loosened and I was able to fit the wrench over the lug nuts of the wheel. Using all my strength, I cracked the lug nuts loose.

The jack was also frozen with disuse. It creaked horribly as I jacked up the car and took the wheel off. I put the lug nuts on the ground, where they were immediately blown around by the wind. The car swayed. I jumped out of the way as the jack assembly collapsed and the car went down.

The second time I jacked up the car, I was able get the spare tire on before the car could fall. Now the lug nuts were missing. I searched the road. I went down into the roadside ditch and sifted through piles of leaves and dead tree branches. Sounds were coming from the woods. Branches were snapping and leaves were rustling even after I stopped moving. What animal or ghost was out there?

I found only two of the lug nuts in the ditch, so I removed a lug nut from one of the front wheels and put three on to the rear wheel. Three and three seemed safer than four and two.

This time the Toyota started right up. I put the car in gear and drove slowly onward.

I entered a less heavily wooded area where the trees seemed to have been planted in a certain order. There were mailboxes, and metal gates barricading private driveways. The road turned to blacktop with an unbroken yellow line down the center. The signs of orderly life reassured me, and I wanted to believe I was entering Delia's neighborhood. But I was still lost. Despite the better road, the Toyota began to rattle as the rear tire wobbled. I heeded the warning of the missing lug nuts and slowed down. Finally, I reached an open field. I drove off the road and onto the untrimmed grass and weeds. I lay across the backseat of the car and looked out through the window. How close had I come to Hastings-on-Hudson?

The screen door had opened and Delia had called to

someone in the house. From the driveway, from Sal's car, we'd heard her calling.

A wooden fence, broken in several places, bordered the field. I felt completely alone. I didn't hear insects, or birds, or the rustle of mice. No other cars passed.

I thought in fragments, permeated by pain. I couldn't organize my thoughts into any particular pattern. I couldn't have responded to a question or even have fended off a mouse if it had jumped in the car window and landed on my chest. I lay in the backseat of the Toyota and slept fitfully. My anxiety seemed almost palpable.

I dreamed that a phone was ringing. When I answered it, a woman's voice said, "Be waiting outside." Then I was in a hospital elevator going down. A Xerox of a journal article lay in the corner, footprinted. The elevator stopped and the doors creaked opened at every floor, but no one got on.

Outside, the river was as black as the sky. I waited on the street. A jogger approached me. Over his jogging suit, he wore an old fur coat. His face was wrinkled with age, yet his body was muscular. Could it be Rulo? When he reached me, the nostrils of his familiar nose flared wide. "I will prepare you! *Sivis pacem, para bellum.* If you wish for peace, prepare for war!"

Rulo grabbed my hands, as if touching me could save what he said from the evanescence of dream.

"The Luger," he said, "is a handsome gun. It lies so well in the hand. The bullet shoots straight through the head. Such piercing power."

My throat constricted. I wasn't able to speak.

"A second choice is Winchester. The magazine holds nine rounds. The tenth round is in the chamber. Though Luger is inarguably the better weapons. Winchester will not jam. It shoots practically by itself. You almost never have to reaim. And there's a balance, you see, between the weight of the bullet in relation to the charge. The bullet has the lightweight caliber, and so it travels with greater speed. It cuts through the head like a cabbage, wreaking havoc in a man's brain. You know, it's the way they did in a Kennedy."

Rulo spoke in a whisper.

"The Luger is superior to the high-caliber weapons *the brothers* employ when they break your bones and you are carried off by your kneecaps. With Luger, you must adjust your aim. If Kell is running from right to left, you add one meter in the leftward direction, shooting to where he will be at the exact moment the bullet arrives."

He really knows the physics of it, I thought.

"Why thank you, Levy," dream Rulo said, knowing my thoughts. "Remember, this is not a movie, where you may be shot in the shoulder and still you're going. In the modern film, there is all this time for talking. You hold the gun and give the whole silly speech before you fire. In life, someone would be dead before any of it took place—the whole garrulous business, calling Kell a swine, pacing back and forth. In life, you'd get shot yourself, right away; there's your headline story. It's shoot or be shot!"

Rulo laughed harshly. "It is the middle of the night. Someone shrieks at you in Italian. If only you held the ready Luger! *Sivis pacem, para bellum.* The gun says it!"

Rulo's beret fell forward. Ratlike hair rimmed his large ears. His nose, broad and crooked, with the brown mole at the end of it and the two short bristles arising from the mole—the nose drew a sudden breath.

"And all over a woman," he said, as night ebbed all around us and the sky began to lighten. "She will take away your life. She will provoke your emotions, but you must be heedless!"

On the balcony above us, an empty wheelchair was shrouded in shadow. Down here on the street, the shadows were moving. A car passed. Another car turned toward us, its headlights aiming in.

"She sees you," the Rulo jogger said.

The car halted a few feet away from us. The door on the passenger side shot open.

"Get in." I recognized the voice from the telephone call that had told me to wait outside.

I entered the car and we were off, the pressure of the sudden start throwing me back against the seat. A dream BMW could steer itself, its wheels in perfect alignment, its speed held constant. A dream BMW could probably lift itself off the road.

The driver controlled the windows and the dream climate from a panel of glowing buttons on her left. She steered with her right hand, her elbow hooked down around the gearshift. I smelled shampoo and clean skin.

Where was she taking me?

She drove past an open field that smelled of sewage. Sal

Vertino ran alongside the car; the muscles in his legs tensing and untensing. We outdistanced him; soon we were well beyond him.

A train whistle echoed in the distance. Before long, we drove alongside a freight train. The boxcars appeared to be sealed. The train moved haltingly. The cars bumped together like blood against the valves of phlebitic veins.

The train bumped to a stop. Men in blue garb appeared outside it. A man on the train prepared to jump, aiming for our car. The muscles in his legs tensed as he leaped, aiming ahead of where my door was, calculating where it would be when his jump coincided with our car.

But Delia accelerated. I kept waiting for the sound of the man hitting the ground behind us.

Delia kept driving until we were back on the highway and this no longer felt like a dream. We were approaching Bellevue from the north. The police were lined up ahead of us with their flashing lights and rubber cones, and the traffic inched along through a heavy rain. It was still just before dawn. As we approached the site of the accident, I saw the bystanders. They wore yellow rubber coats. They communicated the facts with their eyes to every passing car. I was still in my dream, waking up, having to know the facts, not yet knowing them.

Delia stared out the window. When she turned to me, at first her eyes were unrevealing.

"I didn't know where he was going," she said.

It was dawn.

She stopped the car at the shoulder of the road, and we faced the torn railing. The paltry city grass sparkled with fragments of unbreakable windshield glass.

The BMW's headlights faded in the gray light of morning. The edge of the road became visible. There were no tire tracks or skid marks leading to the hole in the railing.

"You can't be here," a policeman said to us.

I was surprised to hear my voice. "We're doctors," I said.

"It's too late for doctors."

The police had finished releasing flesh from metal with their tools. The body had been taken away, and the remains of a ten-year-old Italian sports car had been hauled off by a tow truck.

Delia and I were strangers, even in a dream. We didn't talk. I hardly knew her. She turned to me. As I began to truly awaken, I thought, *What does her look mean?* I opened my eyes, but I still saw her face. *Would I ever be able to rid myself of this nightmare?*

I said, "Where was Sal coming from?"

Delia said, "I don't know."

But waking to the grayest morning of my life, compressed in the backseat of my Toyota parked in an open field somewhere in an unknown section of Westchester, I knew that in my dream, Delia was lying.

11

By the time I awoke, it was the next day. I'd slept for ten hours in the backseat of the Toyota. I looked out the window at a lifeless field. In the daylight I could see that the grass and weeds were brown and stiff. Animals and insects avoided this patch of land entirely, as if someone had sprayed it with a killer chemical. The stillness reflected my mood. I was depressed. The lower centers of my brain ran my body. If I moved at all, it was only because the controls for breathing and eating were combined with newer reflexes to return to the hospital and draw blood.

I knew I had to rally for Sal's memory, and for myself. When I was back at Bellevue, I would have to endure more scrutiny. The system that spewed out Sal was committed to the belief that those who challenged it were aberrant. I had to reenter the heart of this system and master the skills I needed to doctor. If I succeeded, I would be transformed. But what kind of doctor would I become, working under the ruthless whims of a Kell?

Again, the Toyota started right away. I backed it down the field, then retraced the side roads as best I could until I found a main road. I stopped for gas and directions to the thruway.

I felt better as I drove home. All I had to do to succeed was complete my tasks in a timely manner. Internship required little thinking and even less decision making. I would concentrate on being dependable and staying away from ward politics. Sal had gotten himself caught in a political and romantic tangle that I could easily avoid.

It was 7 A.M. when I exited at Bellevue, following a city ambulance that was shaped like an ice cream truck. It went along quietly without sirens, without its top lights blinking. It didn't appear to be on duty. As the ambulance approached the emergency entrance, a man in the back of the ambulance pressed his face against the greasy window and made an imprint there.

Bellevue was quiet; I parked my car in the parking lot and went inside the main entrance. At the elevators, a warmhearted clerk was handing out coffee to each patient who rolled past in a wheelchair.

Fat Goldman waited for me in the doctors' station. His

eyes were red. He didn't have his soda container or his cigarettes. He wore a dark suit, and his stethoscope bulged in the pants pocket. He hugged me.

According to Goldman, The Boss had already called an emergency meeting of the University trustees to authorize a commemorative plaque for Sal. Meanwhile, several angry nurses were circulating a petition calling for an investigation into Sal's death. Goldman said the combined effect of the one group's pomp and the other group's fury was chaos.

He led me to the dayroom, where a chart rack and folding chairs had been assembled with the haste of a gallows. The chart rack would have to serve the guest speakers as a lecturn.

While the staff assembled in the dayroom, I went to phone Giuseppe. The day before, Goldman had notified him by telephone. Goldman said Giuseppe had acknowledged the news and then hung up the phone. Today there was a recorded announcement at the clinic: The clinic was closed indefinitely. Medical emergencies were referred to a neighboring town. There was no beep, no invitation to leave a message at the end of the announcement.

Dr. Kell was first. He spoke without rancor, asking us all to recall an intern who was conscientious and obedient. He spoke of "ill timing, an unfortunate set of medical and psychiatric circumstances."

Kell's words galled me. His tone was patronizing. As usual, he presented himself as some kind of mental health expert, despite a lack of formal training.

A medical student at the back of the crowd began to weep. Others turned and glared at him. It occurred to me that a medical student was more likely to lose control of his emotions than an intern. In fact, under different circumstances than these, an intern blood-drawing machine might count on his medical student to cry for a dying patient, while the intern was too busy and too numb to respond properly.

I sat with Goldman in the first row. Kell called Goldman's name. Goldman stood up but refused to come forward to the chart rack. Kell's tone was pompous, and Goldman would not accept his mistreatment. My grief had fashioned a nightmarish image of Kell. But even in the light of day, he was despicable.

"Sal was so alive," Goldman said from his seat. "It seems absurd to be doing his eulogy. Many of us were jealous of him. Kell wants you to think he had *the virus*. My ass, *the virus*. The real question is, did we help him, or did we grind him out? I say he was right not to trust us. I say we're accountable for his death. I for one feel I could have prevented it."

Kell gripped the sides of the chart rack and lowered his head. What had his final role been in Sal's demise? I vowed to find out.

Goldman coughed and shifted his feet. The crowd remained quiet as Goldman continued. "I was also jealous of his success with females. I competed with Sal. I didn't treat him fairly."

A small group of patients watched from the side. They

cheered Goldman's concessions, except for one patient who was too sick to know what was going on: Mrs. Ryan slumped forward in her wheelchair, breathing heavily. It was almost impossible for me to accept that she was still alive but Sal was dead.

Delia sat in the second row, directly behind Goldman, though he may not have known she was there. Her hair was uncombed, and she wasn't wearing makeup. Dark sunglasses hid her eyes, and her white coat was crumpled and missing several of its buttons in the front. *The same for her as for Kell,* I thought. Where was she just before the fatal accident? I vowed to find out.

I watched her openly, until she removed her glasses and glared back at me. I could tell that she'd been crying. She seemed affronted, as if I'd invaded her privacy just by looking at her. But as she continued looking, a flicker of curiosity seemed to keep alive her interest, as if I could become an extension of Sal somehow, and serve as a surrogate for her unresolved feelings. Just the hint of this, whether I was imagining it or not, horrified me. Even as she looked away, and didn't look again, I'd already been given the fuel for nightmares to come.

From the third row, an elderly man spoke with a thick European accent. The entire crowd tensed from his first word, knowing he was The Boss.

"Our fathers were tailors," he said, "so we could be doctors. We must not question. We must work until we learn to do it right."

Goldman turned all the way around and frowned directly at The Boss. But The Boss looked right past Goldman. Perhaps The Boss's eyesight was impaired.

"Dr. Bruner," Kell said. "Would you like to eulogize?"

The Boss gestured with his hands, palms up.

"What is there to say? I know this boy's family. Tragedy stikes every generation. This is unfortunate, but we have to go on."

"How can we just go on?" one of the medical students said.

"We're not tailors," another one said. "Sal's not a suit."

The Boss left his row of seats. When he'd stood up, I remembered how small a man he was—barely over five feet tall. He walked stooped over, hesitating with each step.

I followed him. "Wait," I called, as The Boss hobbled away. He didn't respond to me. I wondered if he could hear me. Did he recall our meeting in the hallway?

Kell joined The Boss, taking his arm and helping him down the hall. The official gathering was now an official farce. It had barely started, but it was over. Everyone began to leave. The other speakers automatically canceled themselves now that The Boss had left the gathering. Sal's high school football coach, his medical-school advisor, the director of Bellevue nursing—all followed the crowd out.

"You bastard, Kell," I shouted, but Kell also disregarded me. I was afraid to go after them, afraid to confront them. I reasoned that I was protecting my career, yet I loathed myself for being a coward. I did my lashing out from a safe distance when it was already too late to make an impact.

* * *

Sally Wilson helped me to interpret my dream. We met, the night after Sal's death, in the same café where we'd had our first date. In addition to being a nurse, Sally also had a degree in psychology, and her empathy was the first comfort I'd felt in more than a day. We sat at the same window table, and she held my hand. I sipped from a cup of coffee until it grew cold and the waiter began to eye us with frustration.

"Mr. Rulo is your friend," Sally said. "You look to him for guidance. Maybe you think he can really walk, or maybe his muscular appearance in the dream has to do with Sal."

"What about the Luger?"

"It's your hostility over the pointlessness of Sal's death. You want to fight back against the authority that helped bring him down. Maybe you think Kell was responsible, or maybe he just represents the institution."

"I think Kell was responsible," I said evenly. "And Delia."

"In the dream you do. You certainly think she knows more than she's admitting. You're very aware of the way the men compete for her, risking themselves as the other muscular man does, jumping recklessly from the train."

"Isn't he Sal too?"

"He's any of you."

"Not me."

Sally shrugged. "Maybe yes, maybe no."

"What do you think the train represents?"

"That's very interesting. Cars, trains, boats represent motion away from death, almost as though by keeping moving and keeping awake you can keep away from death. At the same time, there is always the danger inherent in the vehicle, as Sal's accident shows."

I looked at Sally with growing respect.

"Before Sal died, I had a dream that he was leaving in a sailboat. Maybe that was a warning. Then he called me, right before the accident, and I could tell how distraught he was, yet I didn't do anything."

"You didn't know where he was. Whether he was a suicide or psychotic or under pressure to escape his pursuers, what could you have done?"

I nodded, wishing I could agree. I paid for the coffee, leaving more tip than the waiter was expecting. I followed Sally out of the café, glad when she invited me back to her apartment.

I never would have made it through the weeks that followed if it hadn't been for Fat Goldman. As July gave way to August, and the first six-week rotation finally neared its finish, Goldman guided me through. His entire personality seemed to have changed. Overcxome by guilt and remorse, he was as devoted as he'd once been derisive. He worked with me on all my patients, drawing blood like an intern, collecting supplies, checking results. He became my teacher, explaining every patient-care decision, every change in medication. He praised me for becoming more organized, forgave me for being distracted. He was bombarded by telephone calls from Kell—Is Levy working? Can he handle his tasks? Should he be suspended? Goldman protected me. Kell scheduled daily attending rounds, but Goldman repeatedly canceled them. Soon he wasn't answering Kell's pages.

Kell entered more and more of my patients into his study. A week after Sal's death, a red bag hung over almost every bed, but Goldman removed the mysterious liquid wherever he found it. The next day the bag would be back again, and Goldman would remove it again.

Goldman paid for his assertions with his hard-earned privileges. His rank was stripped from him a bit at a time. Soon he no longer functioned as a chief resident. Scheduling, teaching, and administrative chores were all handled by the other chief residents without Goldman's input.

Two weeks after Sal's death, Goldman and I stood in the doctors' station at 8 A.M. and prepared to make rounds. He wore a freshly pressed doctor's coat, a clean shirt, a new silk tie, and a pair of oversized intern's white pants that he said the hospital tailor had custom made for him three years before. He was still my resident, but he had applied for transfer to a program in California. If accepted, he would complete his chief-resident year there and stay on as a private attending. The hospital had a swimming pool, a sauna and tennis courts, and a private-practice plan for the attendings, with plenty of time off.

"No more crazy women," he said. "I'll get married to a caring nurse and we'll have some babies."

I looked at Goldman, leaning against the wall glass of the doctors' station without his cigarettes or his two-liter soda container. Over the past two weeks, he'd treated me decently, and I'd slowly come to trust him. Still, I recalled his earlier cruelty.

"What about Delia?" I said. "Are you over her now?"

He winced. "To think one woman is the reason for so much suffering."

"Did you have sex with her?"

"Of course."

"How was it?"

Goldman looked at me, narrowing his eyes.

"Levy. However it was, it wasn't worth it."

A nurse with red hair, one of Sal's friends, came to the doctors' station and announced that Larcombe was no longer breathing.

"Again?!"

We followed her to Larcombe's room, where a bag of the study liquid was hanging on an IV pole over his head.

"Obviously he didn't consent to this," I said.

Goldman sighed, the sound of air going out of a large

life raft. "What the hell is he studying? What's he doing to these patients?"

Goldman ripped the red bag off the pole, while I examined Larcombe.

"He's alive."

"How can you be sure?" the nurse said tensely.

"Levy knows him," Goldman said, and the nurse immediately relaxed. Nurses always knew who the good doctors were. In Fat Goldman's case, no matter how mean he'd been before, and no matter how scandalized he was now, his word remained gospel.

Sally Wilson tried to console me, and she was not entirely unsuccessful. My bereavement was so intense I didn't have the stamina for formal dates. So Sally sought me out in the hospital in between her shifts. She kept me company while I did my work. Her presence was soothing to me, and I'm not sure I could have continued to function if I hadn't had these brief trysts with Sally to look forward to.

She met me in the Bellevue coffee shop, tapping me on the shoulder as I waited on line at the take-out. She visited me in patients' rooms. She waited for me in the doctors' station. She even met me down in the X-ray department, where it was becoming almost impossible to get a patient x-rayed.

"The patient's been here for months."

"We have no record," the clerk said.

"Check for it under his first name."

"Look, my coffee break is coming up."

"Try Peter, or Henry."

"There's one under a Zito. Rouleaux."

"Let me see it," I said.

"You can't. It's restricted."

"Who restricted it?"

"I can't tell you."

"Is it something to do with Kell's study?"

The clerk eyed me suspiciously. "If you don't know the answer to that, why are you here looking for it?"

"Because he's my patient!"

"Don't raise your voice with me."

I was enraged. "First you can't find the fucking thing, then you say it's restricted, but you won't say who restricted it!"

"I'm going to have to report you."

"What's one more report," I said evenly.

Now Sally Wilson arrived. As soon as she came to the counter, the clerk began to ogle her.

"It's good to see you around here again."

I explained to Sally that the clerk was withholding Rulo's X ray.

"Please let us see it," Sally said. "The patient's quite ill."

"Sure," the clerk said. "No problem."

Sally put her hand on my shoulder as we walked to the elevator carrying the X ray.

"You must hate this place," she said.

* * *

We were on the roof. We were kissing. We were running our hands through each other's hair. Sally licked my ears. I kissed her in places I wished she would kiss me. When I kissed her ears, she sucked in her breath.

Our coffees were on the floor of the roof. Sally's cup had a lipstick stain on the side of it. I kicked the cup over by mistake, and the coffee was absorbed into the gravel.

It was a beautiful afternoon, cool for the end of July. Rulo called this place Paradise. As if to demonstrate his view, the sun moved out from behind a cloud and reflected off the University Hospital glass on the other side of the river.

We kissed necks, ears. I grabbed her scrub shirt and lifted it over her head. She unhooked her bra and removed it. I kissed the lipstick-colored nipples of her breasts.

She smiled and said, "Here?"

I looked for a place that wasn't all gravel.

But the only urgent rhythm was my beeper going off. I tried to ignore it. Sally put her arms around my neck and pushed her breasts up close to my face. I snaked one hand under her belt. With my other hand I caressed her nipples.

The beeper sounded again, and then again. I thought of silencing it by taking the battery out of its bottom or throwing it off the roof, but Sally was already putting her bra back on. Our stay in Paradise was ending. It wasn't that she was embarrassed. It was just that an experienced nurse like Sally Wilson took the repeated blast of a beeper far more seriously than an overwrought intern like me could imagine.

Sally and I parted at the elevators; it was time for her to start her shift down in the ER. She kissed me and promised to page me in a few hours. As soon as the elevator door closed and she was away, I felt vacant.

My page was about the two housekeepers. When I got to their room, they were screaming and pointing to two IV poles that held bottles of the red liquid.

"We didn't sign for this," one of them said.

"What's this stuff do?" the other one said. "What illness does it treat?"

"I don't know. What illness do you have?"

"Who authorized this?"

"Dr. Kell," I said.

"Couldn't have been Kell," one of the housekeepers said.

"We can have him murdered," the other one said, and they both laughed harshly.

I removed the study equipment from their room and left it out in the hallway.

It was several hours before I could see Sally again, and in that time my emptiness was likely to expand to hopelessness. The monotony of an intern's life was becoming unendurable. I decided it was time for me to visit The Boss. The chart-rack memorial had been a poor time to judge his response. Perhaps he was secretly rooting for me. He had impressed me with his humanity once before. If I spoke with him directly, and he offered me his encouragement, I would have an impetus to continue working. Already, several of my phone calls to his office had not been returned, but why couldn't I just walk in there and knock on his door?

East One, The Boss's office, was a suite of rooms located in a remote corner of the medical ward. I didn't think anyone observed me going there. I opened the outside door and entered without knocking. Just inside, a woman wearing a white lab coat sat behind a gray metal desk. She sanded her fingernails with an emery board. When I announced my name, she spoke briefly into an intercom. Then, without looking at me, she jotted something on a sheet of memo paper, handed it to me, and pointed to a large wooden door. There were unoccupied desks piled high with papers on both sides of this door. It was hilarious to think that with clerks controlling every corridor of the hospital, it was possible to visit The Boss by simply knocking on his door.

I knocked on the door.

"Come in, Dr. Levy," a woman's voice said from inside.

The room was carpeted in red. There was a large mahogany desk at the center and black endowed chairs in the corners. Photographs and plaques hung on the walls. An older woman, her hair saloned into a bun, sat behind the desk. "Dr. Kell will be here shortly," she said, accepting the other woman's memo without looking at it.

"Dr. Kell? I'm looking to speak to Dr. Bruner."

She considered me with the most fleeting of glances. "Do you have an appointment?"

"No. But I was hoping to see him briefly."

"I'm afraid that's not possible."

"Why not?"

The woman stood, collected a stack of papers from the desk, and exited the room without looking at me again.

There was another wooden door toward the rear of the room. I had a sudden impulse to open it and dart into the next room. Perhaps I could encounter The Boss before he could sneak away. I pushed open the door and peered into the room. There was plusher, redder carpeting and larger endowed chairs. Every inch of wall was covered with a photograph or a commemorative plaque. But my expectation wasn't met. There was no one in the room, no briefcase on a chair, and no wrinkled lab coat hanging on a hook.

Someone coughed.

Dr. Kell had come in behind me and was sitting at the mahogany desk, writing in his notebook. He wore his most official lab coat, and it was buttoned to the top button. His name was embroidered in red silk on the sleeve. When he saw that I was staring at him, he removed his spectacles and placed them on the desk.

"Sit down," he said.

I approached the desk but remained standing.

"Where is Dr. Bruner?" I demanded.

"It's better for you if he isn't directly involved."

"Why?"

"Don't be defensive. It's obvious why." Kell smiled his frozen smile and gestured graciously at the red-cushioned chair directly across the desk from him. But I continued to stand.

"I understand you have a problem with the study."

"The housekeepers wanted out. So I let them out."

"I'm not talking about the housekeepers."

"What exactly are you studying, Dr. Kell?"

"That's confidential information."

"Did Sal know what it was?"

Kell tried to stare me into sitting. Failing this, he faked another smile.

"I suppose you expect me to discuss Vertino with you," he said.

"I don't expect anything from you. I'm not sure why you're here. I told you. I want to see Dr. Bruner."

"And I told you. Dr. Bruner will not see you." Kell scanned his notes. "You're frequently late. You're prone to outbursts of temper. You can't take direction. You won't accept criticism—"

"Not according to Dr. Goldman."

"—you're paranoid about the clerks, about half the nursing staff, and about me."

"Where were you when Sal died, Dr. Kell?"

As soon as I asked the question, I wondered why I hadn't asked it before. I had serious questions about his role in Sal's death, about Delia's role, and yet I hadn't pursued them to find out. In fact, I'd been avoiding them for several days. Why? Clearly I'd been afraid of what I might find out, afraid that the knowledge would interfere with my ability to continue to work here.

Kell squeezed his spectacles until his hands reddened. Then he tapped the spectacles against the desk as if he were cracking an egg.

"David, you need help. It's not too late for you."

"What did you do to Sal!? Was it the red liquid?"

Kell laughed. "Ridiculous."

I had the feeling that Kell was toying with me. At the same time that he was reading my responses, his thoughts remained unknowable to me. The combination was unbearable.

"Let me speak to The Boss!"

Kell twisted his hands together.

"You're in trouble, David. You're not functioning. You're up on the roof, bothering the nurses. You're down in X ray, harassing the clerks. You need help. Accept it."

"The roof?"

Horrified by the extent of Kell's surveillance, I backed away from the desk.

"You can't leave," Kell said, squinting at me. "I haven't dismissed you."

I opened the door. In the outer room of East One, the secretary was still filing her nails and didn't seem to notice me.

"David, I may have to suspend you. You're behaving just like your friend."

There was a change in the face of stony authority. I saw a sadistic flicker in Kell's expression. He relished the idea of suspending me. Suddenly my anger overcame my concern for my career. I could no longer restrain myself.

"Fuck you, Kell!"

I slammed the door, anticipating immediate suspension.

Delia was in the anteroom, sitting on a folding chair just beyond the door. I almost didn't recognize her. She wore a long black dress, and her hair had been frosted auburn red, shortened, and fashioned into a bun.

"David," she called to me as I passed, her voice cajoling.

I was too agitated to answer.

Three weeks after Sal's death, I walked up the highway entrance ramp, ignoring the cautioning horns of passing drivers.

Where on the highway had he stopped to call me?

They're coming to kill me . . . Oh God, I'm so afraid.

Why hadn't I found a way to keep him on the phone?

At the accident site, a few shards of glass and the hole in the railing were all that remained. I looked for skid marks, but if they'd been here, they'd been washed away by rain, or rubbed off slowly by passing cars. Examination of the wreck had revealed no evidence of mechanical failure, and the police doubted that Sal had used the brake.

He must have been driving in the left lane going eighty, or even ninety miles per hour. Was he hypnotized by headlight beams enlarging in his rearview mirror? Was he aiming for the exit, the wall, or just escaping from his pursuer? Was Sal insane, a deliberate suicide, or worse, a victim?

Just before the Bellevue exit, Sal must have veered into the right lane. The wheels of the Alfa hit the edge of the shoulder, and then the car was in the air, rocketing a hundred feet before bursting through the metal railing. A terrible sound was produced for every bystander close enough to hear it.

The paramedics found him on the shoulder, fifty yards past the railing, his face torn by glass, his skull opened by metal, his body broken by the Alfa. Already, he was struggling for every breath like a newborn.

Sal's official funeral service had taken place in Catskill, two days after his death. Kell had denied me permission to leave Bellevue to attend. Now, three weeks later, the clinic clerk answered the telephone and said Giuseppe still wasn't taking calls.

"Tell him it's David Levy."

The clerk replied, "Dr. Levy. He says you should be working."

"I must speak to him."

"He's back seeing patients," the clerk said. "He says you should be doing the same."

Finally, late one night, I managed to reach Giuseppe, but only because he happened to answer the phone himself. When I heard his gravelly tones, it reminded me of the time *before* Sal's death, and I almost couldn't speak. In a choking voice, I told him I might be suspended.

"You're okay," he said gently. "They must be trying to scare you."

"How do you know?"

"Just do your work. The eyes of the public are on them now. They won't do anything to you."

"Dr. Vertino," I said, my voice still uneven. "Sal called me just before . . . I didn't know where he was. How could I have stopped him?"

Giuseppe exhaled into the phone, a long deep whistling sound. He hung up without saying good-bye.

Sally's apartment was on the twentieth floor of the Mayfield Apartments. Her windows faced toward Bellevue. Max, her dalmatian puppy, spent most of his time in Sally's bedroom, perched on a wicker basket, paws gripping the sides as he peered through the window and panted. I didn't think a dog could see as far as Bellevue.

I lay naked in Sally's bed, with my head resting on her oversized stuffed bear. I closed my eyes and dreamed of University Hospital: intravenous and blood-drawing teams that did it all for you; lab technicians no one ever saw who withdrew their samples from the bottom of the vacuum chutes. I dreamed about a man on the street who was unaccustomed to the light. Was he a University technician? Was that glove powder chafing his hairy hands?

At Bellevue, the blood-drawing team kept a list of five patients with usable veins. I dreamed that Delia Meducci went from room to room with a tray of supplies, drawing blood from my patients and placing their IVs. She completed all my assignments, checked off the boxes on my lists, discarded the old lists and made new ones. She defended me in my war against the clerks, slowing the pace of their reports. She whispered about me to all the nurses, and now they smiled when they saw me. The more Delia did to help me, the more I knew I could never say no to her.

The beeper was going off. I couldn't stop it from sounding and sounding. I pushed the silence button, turned the off switch, removed the battery, but the dream beeper was still beeping until Sally shook me awake.

Max was sleeping in his basket, which cast a long shadow on the wall. Sally and I lay on top of the covers. I was still naked. She wore an old terry-cloth robe that came open as she turned toward the nightstand. She seemed to anticipate the phone ringing, which it did a moment later with the suddenness of a beeper.

Max began to bark.

"Hello. Hello?"

Sally put the receiver down.

We were undefended against the possibility of the phone ringing again.

"I said hello, but no one was there."

"Maybe it was a wrong number."

"It was that woman."

"Which woman?"

As my lover, Sally was intuitively suspicious.

"David, she's crazy and she frightens me. Please stay away from her."

"I will," I promised. Neither of us mentioned Delia's name.

Sally hugged me. She stroked my back, but as we began to make love, the phone rang again.

It rang all night through in my dreams.

"How did you get this number?"

"Meet me."

"You're crazy."

"I must see you."

"What about Sally?"

"It's you and me," the woman's voice said.

When I awoke there was a warm body curled up next to me. Opening my eyes, I saw that it was Max. Sally slept on the other side of the bed. I reached across Max to Sally. She resisted me, as if she knew my dream.

It was the 15th of August. The first six-week rotation was finally ending. From the beginning of July until the middle of August had seemed like a year. It was hard to believe that it had all started with Sal and me and the medical students huddling around the chart rack, waiting for Fat Goldman.

With a new rotation coming up, I was being reassigned to a teaching service, with a competent resident who was eager to work with me. Goldman had arranged this with the other chiefs, using whatever influence he still had left. Goldman said he'd clued them in that I was really a decent, hardworking intern.

Goldman was leaving Bellevue soon. He was going to that hospital in California. His last days at Bellevue were my best by far. I managed to place several IVs in drug abusers. Only the finest interns could reach a drug abuser's sordid veins. I ordered all the appropriate tests, executing Goldman's therapeutics religiously until all my patients began to look good on paper. Still, Goldman received memo after memo from Kell threatening my suspension. Goldman tore them all up, promising that even after he left, nothing would happen to me. During Goldman's last days, I experienced a hint of what it might be like to be a normal intern training in a normal hospital. The clerks allowed me past their checkpoints without confrontation. The nurses smiled at me, though less suggestively than in my dream.

Delia didn't come to our doctors' station, and I didn't see her in the hallways. Sometimes I was in a rage to confront her. Most of the time I was afraid.

I spoke with Sally every day, but we didn't plan another date until the following week. We left several warm, loving messages on each other's answering machines. Looking forward to seeing Sally was my panacea. It helped me with my grief, and it kept me from hating Bellevue.

On Friday afternoon, I said good-bye to Fat Goldman in the doctors' station. Over the past few weeks he'd lost several pounds, and the superior glint had faded entirely from his expression. He no longer smoked, but now he coughed, as if the cigarettes had somehow protected him while he smoked them.

I said, "That woman ruined Sal, and she almost ruined you."

Goldman leaned against the wall glass and looked at the ground. Our last few weeks together, obsessing over the details of doctoring, we'd been buffered from Sal's death. The daily rigors of medicine subverted my grief. Sometimes it seemed as if Sal's life were part of a distant past that I could no longer connect to. Then, other times, moments in the Crash Room recurred, and I was paralyzed with woe.

"It could have been me," Goldman said. "I chose the same path. I felt the first slip and I thought, *This is the excitement.* I dared myself to go on. I knew the chance I took with her. But I took it. And so did Sal, only he slipped again. With no one there to help him, he slid. He went down, all the way down. He couldn't get back out."

The doctors' station was hot. Goldman and I were both sweating. Outside, it was one of the coolest days of the summer. Inside, Bellevue's heaters were on.

"I tried to destroy him," he said. "I should have saved him."

My hand slipped with sweat as I shook Goldman's hand. We parted friends.

PART FIVE

IN EXILE

August 16th

12

When Goldman left Bellevue, I was left unprotected. The effect was immediate. I was supposed to be reassigned to the teaching service, but now, on the posting outside the chief residents' office, my name was crossed off beside the prestigious East Ward team and scribbled in next to the Pain Elective. "Pain" was widely considered to be the worst assignment. The pain service was an outpost of the medical service, located ten floors below medicine, in a back corner of the rehab ward. Pain attendings were former medical attendings who had failed to provide adequate care. Pain patients were mostly terminal cases who no longer responded to standard medical treatments. Pain interns and residents were medical interns and residents banished for their ineptitude. And a rotation on the pain service did nothing to hone an intern's skills. When he or she returned to the medical floor, the outcast intern was bound to be bewildered and disoriented, a target for further ridicule.

The remaining chief residents refused to discuss my assignment to pain with me. I was barely able to glimpse the old couches and the steel desks of the chiefs' office before they ushered me out, saying, "We have nothing to do with it. It's Dr. Kell's decision."

I was very apprehensive. Improving my skills as a doctor was my best defense against abuse, and it might not be possible on the pain service. I envisioned my pain rotation, with nothing to distract me, living in isolation, consumed with grief over Sal and my own uncertain future. Sal would surely have been exiled here if he'd lived.

Kell didn't return my telephone calls. I went to East One, but this time the secretaries said that both Dr. Bruner *and* Dr. Kell were unavailable. There were no memos with my name on them. The door to the inner office was locked.

The first thing I noticed about the pain ward was that there were a lot of foreign patients and they all seemed to be enrolled in Dr. Kell's study. Red liquid dripped down into the veins of the uncomprehending. It was difficult for me to believe that Dr. Kell had provided consent forms in the necessary languages.

At 10 A.M. on August 16th, I rounded for the first time with the permanent pain attending. Dr. Drew was an emaciated man with loose folds of skin around his eyes. He wore rumpled clothes, blew his nose into an old red handkerchief; and chewed gum, which he spat onto alcohol-swab packets that he tossed onto the floor. The resident on the service was Angela Santana, a chubby woman who seemed quite intelligent. She said she'd been sent to pain in lieu of the fast track to chief residency because she was always challenging the higher-ups.

"I don't take their shit," she said. "I refuse to kowtow to the male deviants in authority."

There was no chart rack, so we stood in the hallway. Dr. Drew commented on the patients as they limped by us. Dr. Santana objected to labels that sounded like they'd been taken directly from a book of bigoted humor. Dr. Drew's "colloquialisms of pain" were particularly vile, though he insisted they were based on formal medical concepts. A Hispanic woman with a cane, jittering "Ay, ay, ay," was followed by a Hasidic man with a walker, moaning "Oi, oi, oi." Dr. Drew stated, "These patients are exhibiting fundamental forms of tachycardia known as Ay tach and Oi tach."

Dr. Drew taught us the word for pain in every conceivable language. For the Chinese it was *tung,* for the Hispanics, *dolor.* Hispanic pain on one side of the body was *hemi dolor,* according to Dr. Drew.

Two obese foreigners hobbled up to us.

"Husband-and-wife team," Drew said.

"Please," the woman begged Dr. Drew. "Please."

Drew shrank back against the wall. The man rubbed his belly and moved closer.

"We don't treat stomach pain here," Dr. Drew said weakly. "Stomach pain is a medical diagnosis."

"I treat it," declared Dr. Santana. The patients turned toward her, which gave Drew the chance to wriggle away. I read their wrist tags—Boodhoo Gunrag. Gunga Dunga.

"I'll get a translator," I said.

"Broken English is their only language," said Drew.

Drew allowed Santana to stay with these patients but insisted that I continue with him on his wretched rounds.

At the end of the hall, in semiprivate room 101, with a futile view of the river, an unresponsive man stared at the ceiling. Morphine, a clear liquid, hung in an IV bag over his bed. Had Larcombe been transferred to the pain ward just to torture me? How could anyone tell if he were in pain? I would be compelled to monitor him as he sweated the narcotic sweat. He had no vital signs, so I would have to examine his eyes, measuring the shrinking size of his pupils. It would be my job to keep Drew from killing him. After all, we had never killed him up on medicine, despite the full furor of multiple cardiac arrests.

The same black magnetic chess set lay open by Larcombe's new bedside. The small pieces were assembled in the starting position for a game.

Larcombe remained oblivious to his surroundings.

But he wasn't a demented ninety-year-old who moaned through the night and upset the slumbering nurses. Why torture him with the needles of pain relief?

"Where's the pain?"

"There must be pain," Drew said. "This is the pain service."

"There is no pain."

"But the guy's a dump from medicine. He must have cancer or *the virus*. They all do."

Drew seemed offended. He had been at Bellevue for several years. Pain was his domain, and two inexperienced trainees were contesting everything he said. Probably most of the interns and residents exiled here were content to slide their way through a meaningless rotation.

"According to the nurses you increase his morphine every day."

"Because he's not improving."

"How can you tell?" I asked.

"An imbecile can tell he's not in *less* pain."

"But you're affecting his blood pressure. You could kill him."

"He has no blood pressure."

"What are you talking about. No one's alive without a blood pressure."

"Do you see it recorded anywhere?"

"What if he dies?" I asked, and Drew seemed relieved at the thought.

"No one dies here. If he gets any sicker, I send him right back upstairs."

Lacking clinical judgment, desperately overmatched by anything more than a hangnail, Drew was famous throughout Bellevue for ordering a gallium scan on every sick patient. This three-day test used a radioactive isotope to identify sites of inflammation or infection in the body. The gallium scan never provided a definite diagnosis, but the results were often positive, and Drew arranged for many patients to be wheeled from the nuclear medicine department directly back up to the medical floor. The pain intern was responsible for injecting every patient with the isotope, since the nuclear medicine technicians were forbidden to do so by their powerful union. The prior pain intern warned me that he still glowed in the dark at night. Fortunately for me, during my tour of duty on pain, the gallium scanner was broken.

After the first day, Angela and I rounded alone. We created our own patient charts and filled them with medical data, priding ourselves on keeping the patients too healthy for the gallium scanner. We were a medical service in exile. Our daily rounds were academic. "Pain is the greatest teacher," Angela said, and we studied the physical manifestations of prolonged pain. Angela made frequent references to the medical literature, and she taught me more than I'd learned from Fat Goldman.

Drew spent his days in the pain doctors' station, reading the daily newspapers. He tore out health-care articles and taped them to the wall glass. Santana insisted that these articles were simplifications and distortions of studies in medical journals that Drew had never read.

Drew was terribly afraid of patients' families. He called them "land mines" and avoided his responsibility to keep them informed. When he was cornered, he would nod his head sagely and say, "Doing good, doing good." When he was asked a direct question on patient management, he would reply, "We're working on it."

After my first week on the pain service, Drew began spending most of his time in the poolroom, leaving the daily decisions to Santana.

After two weeks on pain, I developed an unexpected complacency. I wasn't on call at night, and I had no real patient assignments, so I was able to go home before sunset and return well after sunrise. Weekends I was off, and I spent them going to movies, museums, and restaurants with Sally Wilson. My clothes were rarely stained with blood or Betadine anymore, and I shaved and showered every day. Most importantly, I slept eight hours every night and spent my days feeling calm and rested.

But then after three weeks on pain, I began to grow restless. Santana's teaching stimulated me and kept me from obsessing over Sal, but at the same time I felt isolated from the other interns. When they saw me in the lobby or in the elevator, the other interns ignored me, as if I were a soldier in disgrace, having drawn desk duty while they remained in combat. They talked with each other in disease-fighting terms that I longed for as soon as I heard them. Even in the days when I'd been ridiculed as part of the only nonteaching team, I'd still felt vital, I'd still retained responsibility for patients. On pain, everything was academic. When patients destabilized, often they were transferred to medicine or died before Angela or I knew about it. This aspect of the pain rotation was particularly demoralizing. The upstairs intern and resident who received the sick patient never called us to be updated. They must have assumed we had nothing to contribute to the case.

Angela didn't seem affected by this apparent slight. "A patient's a patient," she said, and she continued to provide consummate medical care to all our patients, some of whom were just as sick or sicker than their counterparts on medicine. Angela was interested only in being the best doctor she could be.

As part of her project to clean up the pain service, Angela fought against Kell's study as vehemently as Goldman had. But here Dr. Drew intervened. I wondered if Drew received a commission from Kell for his work. He ordered the nurses to put the bag of study fluid right back as soon as we'd removed it from a patient's room.

Next, Angela created a study within a study, compiling her own data to see if she could prove that the study patients were being harmed by Kell. Unfortunately, weeks of painstaking work didn't prove this. It was impossible to know whether Kell's study was killing the patients, as opposed to their own terrible disease.

As my exile passed the month mark, I could no longer

picture what Kell looked like, and I rarely thought about Delia. I had vowed to investigate them, but pain was too isolated, and I was too troubled. From the stormy mental seas of pain, with Angela as my only life raft, I worked to preserve my sanity. I promised myself that someday I would confront Delia and Kell, but this was not the right time.

At the end of six weeks on the pain service, Angela and I journeyed upstairs to the chief residents' office, where we discovered that our next rotation was also the pain service.

"Dr. Drew will keep us here forever," she said. "So he can play pool all day."

"It wasn't his decision," I said knowingly.

Once again, the chief residents refused to discuss my assignment, and telephone calls to Dr. Kell were not returned. Angela and I sent a series of protest memos to The Boss, but we didn't receive a single reply.

We worked in pain on into October. Larcombe's new roommate was a cancer patient who moaned the entire day, no matter how much clear liquid was dripped into his veins. His thumb pushed the nurse's call button involuntarily. One day, as I was standing in the nurses' station, the incessant ringing on the call button board suddenly stopped.

"Something's gone wrong with room 101," a pain nurse said crossly. She was well past forty and formlessly obese. Her hair was dyed platinum blond. The nails on her tobacco-stained fingers were bitten down to the nub.

"You need to call a code," she said. This nurse had a way of belittling doctors she didn't like. She obeyed no other doctor besides Dr. Drew, whom she'd known for many years and never questioned. If I didn't call a code, she would probably report me to Drew faster than a *virus* biter could lower a Larcombe guardrail.

But I knew this nurse had poor medical judgment and tended to react hysterically to the smallest problem. I walked slowly down the hall, and she followed me, her legs wobbling, her arms held straight out in front of her in what appeared to be her official position for going to a code.

Both patients were in their beds. I bumped into the table between them. Several pawns shook free of the chess set and dropped onto the floor.

"Call a code!" the nurse insisted.

"Not yet."

She immediately picked up the telephone. "Operator, get me Dr. Drew."

Larcombe looked the same as always, but the cancer patient's breathing was labored. His complexion was very pale and his eyes were closed.

"Does he have a Do Not Resuscitate order?" I asked.

"Which patient?"

As I watched him, the cancer patient stopped breathing. I felt his groin and found a thready pulse, but it quickly disappeared.

"Call a code," I said calmly.

"Call a code! Call a coooode! It's a cardiac arrrreeeest!" the nurse shouted, stomping from the room with dinosauric thuds.

I removed an Ambu Bag from the wall, pushed it against the patient's mouth, and began to breathe him. After two breaths I pumped fifteen times on his chest. This was the official format for one-man CPR. I was the only one in the room, and I felt a strange intimacy with the patient. Taking the pink turban from the bedside table, I covered his head, bald from his multiple cycles of chemotherapy.

The fat nurse returned with the pain cart, which was filled with vials of morphine and Demerol but had none of the cardiac stimulants necessary for running a code. I ordered her to bring me the crash cart instead, but she refused to move. A moment later, Drew was in the room, followed by Santana, several other residents, interns, curious students, and nurses wheeling the crash cart.

The nurses began to assemble intravenous lines on poles over Larcombe's bed. Drew flashed a light into Larcombe's eyes.

"Which patient is it?" Santana asked me.

"Here," I said, motioning to the cancer patient.

"But the other one doesn't have a blood pressure or pulse," a nurse from the ICU insisted.

"Larcombe never has a pulse," I said. "Is he warm?"

"Of course," the fat pain nurse said. "Who would code him cold?"

I continued working on the cancer patient, pumping on his chest. Santana joined me and took charge. Her confident assertions were obeyed by the same interns who'd shunned us in the elevator. One took over the Ambu breathing. Another began to inject the heart stimulants that Santana ordered. The interns occupied positions that were usually occupied by nurses. I was surprised, but the interns clearly respected Santana's prowess. The nurses, on the other hand, continued to hover over Larcombe, ready to code the wrong patient.

The head medical nurse looked around the room for a doctor with more authority than Santana. She recognized Dr. Drew and eyed him disdainfully. "Him? Is he still on staff?"

"Dr. Drew. Which patient should we be coding?" the fat pain nurse shouted.

"Check Larcombe's EKG," Drew mumbled, which initiated another wave of activity, as two nurses removed the EKG machine from the cancer patient and attached it to Larcombe.

"Get that back here!" Santana snapped. But the nurses completed the EKG on Larcombe and brought it to Dr. Drew.

He squinted at it and mumbled something to himself.

"What did he say? What did he say?" the fat pain nurse cried.

Drew hesitated. "Okay. Code's over," he said finally.

"But our patient's got a pulse back," Santana said.

"It doesn't matter. I said to stop *all* codes."

The nurses left Larcombe and huddled around the crash cart, counting supplies. The medical students stayed close to Dr. Drew, anxious to make an impression on this new authority, not realizing that he had no power beyond pain.

"He's breathing on his own," Santana announced.

As he recovered, the cancer patient appeared more lifeless. His mouth opened, assuming the frozen O of muscular arrest.

"His blood pressure's back up to ninety. Levy, you saved him," Santana proclaimed.

At every successful code, someone was named savior, no matter how poor the condition of the surviving patient. I felt proud, though I knew I hadn't done this patient a favor. We had saved an unsavable patient, while in the next bed the nurses had been coding the wrong patient. Suddenly I noticed Delia. She must have come in after the other medical students. It had been several weeks since I'd last seen her. She smiled and winked at me, knowing I was the hero. My response was visceral. I hated her, associating her with Sal's death. Nevertheless, I followed her out into the hall.

"Come back here, Levy," Santana called after me.

I was hypnotized by the slide of the gluteus muscle sheathing and unsheathing in Delia's behind. When she faced me, I instantly relearned the bones of her neck and chest and the high angles of her face. I'd forgotten how dark her eyes were. I could tell that her hair had just been fashioned—it was a web of tight curls.

Angela moved in between us. "We're going to round now. You'll have to leave," Angela said. Delia shrugged and walked away. When she reached the end of the hall, she turned and smiled at me' reminding me of the way she'd teased Sal. She disgusted me, yet I was curious.

"What are you doing?" Angela whispered. "Stay away from her."

"I want to talk to her about Sal."

"What's she going to say? You think she'll tell you she had something to do with it?"

"I think she's ready to talk about it."

That night I was called in as sick-call to cover for an intern who had the flu. It was the first time I had been allowed to be on call since being banished to pain. It didn't occur to me at the time that my chance meeting with Delia had something to do with the opportunity. I was so happy to finally be back upstairs even if it was only as a fill-in. I put on my old sneakers and the intern whites stained with Betadine, and I felt the identification returning. I was ready to draw blood. I was ready to round. If only for one night, I would leave the halls of pain and return to the medical floor.

I entered the on-call rooms for the first time in several weeks. It wasn't the same. Goldman's paraphernalia—his cigarettes, soda containers, and Xeroxes were all long gone. Delia sat on Goldman's couch, holding her head in her hands. She was weeping. She didn't seem to know I was there.

"Delia," I said.

She looked up at me, and I saw that her makeup was smeared. Her large eyes were full of tears.

"They were pressuring Sal. He was so weak, so dependent."

Several weeks had passed since his death, yet we were locked into it again, as if it had just happened.

"You betrayed him."

"He clung to me. I was afraid."

"Why are you grieving now?"

She looked quickly around the room. She didn't seem certain we were alone. Would she end up crazy like her mother?

"That day, Delia. What happened to him?"

"I don't know. I wasn't there."

"Where was he?"

She held out her hands to me. The polish had worn off her fingernails, but I could still make out the red color. She seemed miserable, but I wouldn't hold her hands. And she didn't say anything more about Sal.

It never occurred to me that Delia might be responsible for my return to active duty. At the time, I attributed my good fortune to Kell being out of town on a drug-study-sponsored vacation. I was repeatedly assigned as the sick-call intern. And though the gallium scanner had long been fixed, I wasn't required to inject a single patient.

Then Delia began to actively pursue me, as if I were a salve for her newfound suffering. She brought coffee to the pain doctors' station, and paged me throughout the day. When I didn't answer her pages, she returned to the doctors' station and waited for me to come.

"I just want to talk," she insisted when she saw me.

But she still refused to answer my questions about Sal. I followed Angela's advice and stayed away from Delia as much as I could.

She began to wear designer clothes and accentuating makeup. By the final week of the rotation, the page operator laughed each time she told me who was paging me. "That woman's crazy," the page operator said, and I still didn't answer the pages.

One page came from someone else, and I grew sad when I realized the page operator no longer associated my name with hers—Sally Wilson.

"It's all over the hospital. You're having an affair with that woman."

"It's not true."

"Why don't I see you? You don't call me anymore."

"I'm not myself. I'm depressed."

"Max misses you."

"I'll call you tomorrow," I said.

The following day, my mood was worse, and I didn't call Sally.

The next rotation was coming up, and Angela received a memo informing her that she was being reassigned to medicine. She was happy, but worried when I didn't receive a similar memo. I was petrified. If I were assigned to pain yet again, I would become known as the permanent pain intern. And pain without Angela would be unbearable. She sent a memo to The Boss requesting me as her intern on medicine, but when the new list was posted outside the chief residents' office, my name was back beside pain. A short time later, someone crossed my name off and penned it in next to Angela's medical ward team.

I thanked Angela profusely, but she denied having anything to do with the change.

"Must be Meducci's connections," Angela said, laughing.

13

In mid-December, I received a letter from Giuseppe Vertino. He wrote that he was back to working long hours at the clinic. He had also returned to the river, fishing early in the morning before the clinic opened and late at night after it closed. I imagined shards of ice shaped like fish floating past him as he angrily threw and withdrew his line. I could see him lurching bitterly forward, his hip waders stiff with the cold. Giuseppe hoped I was succeeding at my work; good doctoring, he wrote, was a way to overcome grief.

Giuseppe was right. I thrived as a member of a regular ward team. Angela had developed a method for providing medical care on pain that she transplanted to medicine with hardly a change. Every morning we rounded with the charts, going over problems that had occurred the night before and reviewing the latest test results. Then we went to the patients' rooms and examined the patients. The medical students stayed close to me, waiting to hear what I said on every case. They respected me as Angela's representative. Angela graded them, and they knew that in order to please her they had to please me. Attending rounds took place every day at exactly 10 A.M. Our attending was an easygoing University cardiologist who nodded at our presentations and told us what a great team we were. As a confident intern, I knew what my limits were as well as when I needed to call Angela for help. She and I had an unspoken communication that defined my freedom. I had reached a point in my internship when I was able to dispense certain medicines without hesitation. I used diuretics to successfully combat heart failure, and I ordered inhaled bronchodilators to save patients with life-threatening asthma. If only Sal had known the sensation of bringing a dying patient through to the following morning alive.

After stringing several of these satisfying middle-of-the-night moments together, I felt comfortable enough to join the other interns out by the coffee truck. The harder I worked and the more successful I became, the more the other interns seemed to forget my prior ineptitude. Now I was associated in their minds with Angela, an extremely competent, intelligent resident. This was internship as I'd always envisioned it; you were as good as your resident made you; you worked tirelessly within the scheme that was laid out for you. I proudly received my ration of coffee from the fur-lined-mitten–clad hands of the owner of the Bellevue coffee truck. I huddled before the truck at night, coffee steaming in my cup, a candy bar turning stiff in my lab coat pocket.

The river at night was black and reeked of sewage. Rulo's hellish vision of The Hades—debris and decayed flesh swirling in the dark tide like boats without anchors—made real. Staring at the foul river, I recalled Sal's anguish: Delia and Goldman on the flimsy bed in the corner on-call room, rivers of Goldman's blubber rolling as he grunted and then plunged, pulling back, steadying, followed by another thrust, another plunge. Delia shock absorbing as Goldman humpfed and then slowed.

Delia's current student rotation was psychiatry, but she rarely attended. She claimed that the entire field could be learned in a single week. She vehemently denied any special interest in psychiatry despite her father's reputation or her mother's illness.

She spent her time following me on my rounds. The more I ignored her, the more she followed me. It seemed that she was expecting me to fall into the same trap that she had used to snare Sal, foregoing my work for her. My growing proficiency as a doctor required my constant attention and seriousness. It was imperative that I resist her. But my interest in her importance to Sal began to overwhelm me. It seemed to me that despite my hatred of her destructive antics, I was becoming more and more attracted to her by the simple fact that Sal had loved her. My heart rate increased and I began to sweat whenever she appeared. I kept hoping she would reveal her secrets to me, but I was too nervous to question her further about Sal.

Angela didn't approve of Delia accompanying us. "Where are you supposed to be?" Angela asked her repeatedly. "Who gave you permission to round with us?" Though the rotation was almost over and all our patients were doing well, Angela seemed as worried as I was that Delia's presence would somehow mean my undoing.

Delia began to avoid Angela by coming to the hospital at 7 A.M. and joining me on my pre-rounds. Then she would find me again late in the day, when Angela had already gone home. One early evening in late December, I went to a patient's room to place an IV and found Delia already swabbing his arm with alcohol and Betadine. Though I hadn't given her my permission, she poked the patient repeatedly with the needle catheter. She searched for his vein, and I didn't try to stop her.

"You have to angle it in."

She stepped back from the patient.

"You'd better do it," she said, handing me a new catheter. I took her place, and she stood behind me, her hands tickling the backs of my arms as I pushed the needle beneath the skin. My hands shook, yet somehow there was the *pop* of the needle going into the vein. A drop of blood came back up through the hub of the catheter.

"It's in," Delia announced.

She continued to stand behind me as I taped the catheter down. I felt her breasts brush against my back as I slipped a piece of tape under the hub of the catheter. I folded over the sticky side of the tape, securing the plastic to the patient's skin. I was embarrassed by my erection, which grew larger and harder as Delia pushed her pelvis up against the back of my thighs.

The patient seemed unaware of the sudden sexual excitement. He also didn't seem to know he had a working IV. He turned away, as if he expected to be stuck again with the needle. But I was oblivious to him, losing track of everything except my lust. I rationalized that my interest wasn't romantic. I was a frustrated male responding to the advances of a physically gifted female. We left the patient's room, and Delia led me unresisting to the on-call rooms.

My rage at her ruthless betrayal of Sal gave way to my desire. Frankly, I was curious to see if she was the dynamic lover that Sal had said she was. My hormones overcame the fear I had of losing control of my internship. In fact, I knew I was endangering my job. But the suddenness of Delia's seduction overwhelmed any chance for a rational resistance. I forgot my patients and thought only of reaching the other side of the on-call room door.

Since Goldman's departure, the on-call rooms had devolved into rumpus rooms. Interns and residents from all the services in the hospital supposedly had sex here. Delia and I headed for her favorite corner room. Once inside, she closed the door and turned the lock. We sat on the narrow, sheetless bed. I thought of Sally Wilson, whom I hadn't seen in several weeks. Recently, she had stopped calling me. Sadly, I knew that it was my obsession with Sal's death and now with his lover, as much as the rigors of internship, that had interfered with my enthusiasm for Sally. How long would it be before I regretted letting Sally go?

Delia didn't speak. She put her hands under my scrub shirt and scraped my chest with her long fingernails. She lifted her scrub shirt over her head. She wore no bra, and her large breasts bounced down against her skin as the shirt came off. I put my hands on her breasts. Her fingers roamed my chest as I squeezed her stubby, nickel-sized nipples. She seized my belt. My beeper sounded as she removed it. Had she triggered it accidently? It went off again.

We ignored the page, moving together until the beeper went off yet again.

"Maybe I'd better answer it," I said, but Delia undid my belt and reached into my pants.

"I don't have any condoms," I said.

She smiled, running her tongue along the top of her lips.

"I hate condoms," she said.

We had sex all over the hospital, several times a day, for the next few weeks. I managed to convince myself that there was no great risk of *the virus,* despite the fact that we never used condoms. Anonymously, I consulted our hospital's top epidemiologist, who said that the risk of transmitting *the virus* during a single bout of unprotected sex was somewhat less than one percent.

"Each time?" I asked.

Delia also told me she didn't believe in birth control. "Besides," she said, "I'm probably infertile."

We had sex standing up in the bathroom, on the windowsill in Larcombe's old room, and lying on the floor in the janitor's closet. She climbed on top of me on the narrow bed in the corner on-call room, bucking and thrusting as if I were a mechanical device built solely for her pleasure. I was paged in the middle of a particularly long sex session, and when I finally called back, the page operator said Angela had given up looking for me and had taken care of the patient herself.

I had trouble completing my tasks, and I was often late for rounds, sometimes missing them altogether. I avoided Angela as much as I could, and when I did see her, I refused to admit anything, though I was sure she knew what was going on. Angela could have reported me but she covered for me instead, assuming much of my workload. Surely she was hoping that my affair would be short lived and the old reliable Levy would resurface. But my obsession for Delia had become all consuming. I still didn't admit to real passion, but I did experience a growing self-confidence. It was as if this affair could somehow bring me status as I found myself filling Goldman's shoes.

Actually the affair risked the opposite outcome. The longer it lasted, the longer it took me to answer my pages. Soon all the effort I'd put into rebuilding my damaged reputation would be wasted. Angela couldn't be everywhere at once. All it took was one missed page for the word to spread that the West Ward team was in trouble. Luckily, this didn't happen, and I was able to make it all the way to the final day of the rotation, December 31st, without a major reprimand or an accusatory memo. Then, on the final day, the cardiac arrest beeper went off four times before I answered it. By the time I left Delia in the on-call room and ran to my patient's room, the code was already over.

The red liquid hung in a bag over the patient's head. He wasn't moving, and his pupils were fixed and dilated. His body was stiffening, and his skin was cool and getting colder. Everyone except for Dr. Santana had already left the room. Angela was removing the EKG electrodes. She refused to look at me.

Dr. Kell arrived, accompanied by two nursing supervisors. I hadn't seen Kell in several weeks. He'd clearly lost weight, and he was very pale. But when he saw that the patient was dead, he immediately reddened with anger. "You killed a study patient," he roared at me.

Angela looked at Kell with disgust. "The patient had a bad heart. His liver was failing. He was infected."

"It doesn't matter what he had. Levy's suspended. He's jeopardizing patients' lives. I won't allow you to keep covering for him."

"Levy's a good intern. If anything killed this patient, it was your unethical study."

"What do you know about my study?" Kell said.

Angela refused to answer. Whatever evidence, confirmed or unconfirmed, she had amassed against Kell, Angela was too smart to let him have a glimpse of it prematurely. Angela left the EKG machine and went to the window, seeming more disgusted with Kell than ever.

Delia came into the room and went to the dead patient's bedside. Kell stared at her openly, seeming to forget about the attack on his study. He began to hum a melody to himself.

"Not savable," Delia said, and both nursing supervisors sighed with relief. Delia wore an attending's lab coat, a violation of uniform I'd never seen before at Bellevue. Did the nursing supervisors mistake this arrogant medical student for an attending with greater clout than Kell?

"You're still suspended," Kell said to me.

"Why? There was nothing I could have done."

"You could have been here."

Did Kell know where I'd been instead? I was embarrassed to see that Delia hadn't straightened herself after sex. Her hair was mussed, her makeup was smeared, and her shirt was stretched at the collar from my pulling. It was easy to see her breasts as she leaned over the dead patient. There was a red mark on the left side of Delia's neck. The smell of her perfume and her sweat were still in my nostrils. My groin was sticky and it chafed whenever I moved. The nursing supervisors seemed to be staring at my waist. I had an erection, and looking down, I saw that my zipper was halfway down.

But now Delia was watching Kell as he circled the dead patient like some kind of academic vulture. He scribbled notations in his red notebook. Perhaps he thought he could still salvage data for the study. When Kell left the room, Delia followed him. I went out into the hallway and watched them walk off together; Kell gesturing, Delia laughing.

"Delia!" I called, but just ten minutes after having sex with me, she ignored the sound of my voice.

Angela Santana helped me once again. She prevented my suspension by appealing to a higher authority. Her own reputation was still not entirely secure, yet she used it to protect me. At three o'clock that afternoon, she presented a rare medical case at a last-day-of-the-rotation conference that The Boss attended. The patient had combined albinism, colitis, and lung disease. Angela concluded with a flourish that the diagnosis was rule out Hermansky Pudlock syndrome, an extremely rare genetic disorder. Angela credited Dr. David Levy with having made the diagnosis, and The Boss was clearly impressed. Of course, two hours after the conference it was discovered that the patient was a *bedless* who'd read the medical text, as I had, then bleached himself and drank the bleach and inhaled the fumes in order to gain hospital admission. By the time it was common knowledge that the rule out diagnosis was a hoax, I was already well along in the next rotation, with Angela Santana again as my resident.

Sal Vertino had once insisted that a moment of sexual bliss with the right partner was worth the risk of rejection. But moments after sex, Delia could divert to someone else. The effect of this was excruciating. I'd gotten hooked on her, experiencing what Sal had experienced, plus the fulfillment of my own need to be desired. I'd even loved being reckless, only the more dependent on the sex I became, the more powerless I felt, as if I were no longer established in any way. I'd been counting on a growing intimacy, as if the more we had sex, the more she would reveal to me. Yet, in my infatuation, I'd missed a chance to explore these intimate moments for clues about Sal. How could I have known I would be cast aside so soon? Kell's reappearance signaled a change, and it brought back all the old questions to which I still had no answers. Had Sal gone crazy? Had he been driven from the road, or had he deliberately veered into the next lane, into the next world, having no regrets and leaving not a single skid mark behind him?

On into January, I was unable to complete my work. Angela's confidence and patience with me now seemed foolish. She continued to cover for me, working for days in the new rotation in the role of intern/resident. She grew angrier at my lapses, more irritated by my uncompleted tasks. It wasn't long before she would be compelled to give up on me, promoting a student to subintern until an intern could be reassigned. I was running out of time, but I couldn't stop myself. I thought about Delia constantly. I sought her out, but I couldn't find her. Now *I* was the one having *her* paged five times a day, and *she* didn't answer *me*. She'd recently rented an apartment in Manhattan, and I called there, but there was no answer. Her answering machine didn't have a voice message, just a single beep followed by several seconds of static. I didn't know if the machine was recording, but I left several messages, and she didn't call me back. The telephone number for the house in Hastings-on-Hudson was unlisted. I didn't know the number, though according to Sal's letter, Kell had known it all the way back in July.

I was destroying my career over Delia, but like Sal, I felt I couldn't stop myself. I looked for her in the on-call rooms, in the coffee shop, even on the roof. I waited for her in the poolroom for hours, but she never came.

14

In early January, I received a memo from The Boss:

I regret to inform you that your contract is not being renewed for next year. If you have any questions, please contact Dr. Kell. He will be available to help you, should you desire to continue your residency in medicine at another institution.

Sincerely,
Dr. Bruner

I sat in the doctors' station, drinking one coffee after another while Angela tried to reason with me. She was still sympathetic, but she was also firm in her ideas.

"I'll appeal the decision," she said, "but you'll have to work harder. The woman's a real bitch. You'll have to forget her and concentrate on your work. And it isn't like you two were so close. You, like everyone else, went out with her. Big deal."

I nodded my agreement, yet I remained in the doctors' station after Angela had left. Passing nurses pointed at me through the wall glass. While Angela circled the ward, doing my work plus her own, I lost track of the time and continued to be preoccupied with Delia.

Sometime late in the afternoon, Rulo rolled into the doorway. A glass bottle of the red liquid hung from an IV pole connected to the arm of his wheelchair. When I tried to disconnect him from the IV, he kicked at me with his prosthesis.

"I thought you hated Kell's study," I said. "At University Hospital, you were so glad to be disqualified."

"How else am I to receive care? You know they love to study me, and I, in return, am now the recipient of free food."

"They may be killing you."

"I am killed already. Have you seen my X ray? It is the classic Nietzschean struggle between the savage tar and the accommodating pink pocket of the lung. Oh, the losing battle between the life-giving sponge and a lifetime of contemplatory smoking."

"But you're still smoking," I said. Rulo's shirt pocket bulged with two or three crumpled cigarette packages.

Rulo shrugged. "I am practically extinguished. Every

word I utter instantly becomes entropy. For as long as I remain alive, I witness. I am the hallway patrol. The patients squirm in their unattended squalor."

Rulo kicked his prosthesis against the wall glass of the doctors' station.

"How can you submit yourself to Kell? Are you depressed?"

"I have lost my motion, awoken from my action dreams. I am a creature of the laboratory. I no longer purge myself. I no longer fight. I, Victor Rulo, am now no more than a simple beast. Oh the creaking of the great machine!"

The wart bristles on his nose didn't look human. His tiny black eyes shifted back and forth. He dug his fungus-ridden fingernails into my arm and leaned closer to me. I backed away.

"Victor," I said, "I'll be leaving Bellevue. I've been dismissed."

Rulo seemed sad. "There's still time for you to succeed. You must attain the fortress of indifference. A pistol will not help you. You must steel yourself with the armor of nonchalance."

Rulo kicked a candy bar wrapper away from his wheelchair with a sudden thrust of his prosthesis. Despite all his afflictions, he was rallying on my behalf. How could I continue to wallow?

"Your friend wasn't murdered. There was no fiendish plot. You're becoming just like he was. An intern out of options."

"He was a victim."

"He refused to play by their rules. He was an errant knight, foolishly pursuing the queen."

Rulo grinned his lopsided grin, and I wondered again, was he a soothsayer, or was he a psychotic bum in someone else's discarded clothes? Were his visions hallucinations, his insights nothing more than elaborate guesses? As I walked away from him, he guessed again—rightly—that I was off to look for Delia.

"You must not pursue her," he said. "She is the black widow spider. Am I to forfeit my favorite doctor to her venom?"

I headed for the elevator, feeling stronger. Contrary to Angela's view, and now Rulo's, I was convinced that confrontation was the only way to free myself from my obsession. I saw myself as Sal. And as I faced off with her, somehow I had to avoid Sal's fatal mistake. Had Sal confronted her?

"Be careful," the live Rulo called after me, knowing my thoughts as well as any dream Rulo.

Delia's new apartment was located on Riverside Drive, overlooking Hudson's river. The Toyota brought me to a puttering stop in front of the four-story building. It was at least a hundred years old, and the high-ceilinged lobby looked like the entrance to a church. The mailbox listed just four names, one per floor. Meducci was the name at the top.

The temperature outside was several degrees below

freezing, and there was a brisk wind. I didn't have an overcoat, so I ran from the car to the lobby. Despite the bad weather, the door into the building was open. Inside, wearing wool mittens and a fur hat, the doorman leaned against his post. He eyed me curiously but didn't say anything as I ran across the lobby and entered the stairwell. It was a long climb. Judging from the number of steps between floors, the apartments had very high ceilings.

Climbing the stairs, I was feeling the furious energy of my betrayal. But by the time I reached the top floor, my breath was short, my legs were weak, and my thinking had changed. Maybe I was wrong. Maybe I could still work things out somehow. Maybe she had avoided me because of the sudden intensity of our relationship so soon after Sal's death. If I controlled my feelings, she could become a regular part of my life again. It would be easier for me to work. I would become the intern Angela expected me to become. Delia would respect me more for my success. By the end of the year, The Boss would insist that I stay. I would decline, accepting an offer at a better program uptown.

At the door to Delia's apartment, I hesitated, realizing again how thin my fantasy was. Angela was right. I hardly knew Delia. I could just walk away. Instead, I knocked lightly. When no one answered, I tried the doorknob and it turned. My heart beat rapidly, and the blood circulated my compulsion until I lost control completely. I yanked open the door and stepped forward into Delia's apartment.

* * *

A surgeon controlled his obsession, bearing in layer by fascial layer, tying off bleeders, never looking beyond where he was, never looking back to the skin. He was committed to the entire process from the first cut. He didn't stop to use the toilet. He didn't give up, leaving the patient gutted and bleeding on the table. When he reached the affected organ, a surgeon repaired it, with only the slightest smile. Then he withdrew, layer by fascial layer, repairing with suture what he had rent with the knife.

From the welcome mat just inside the door, I could see into a large parlor. Heads of deer were mounted on the paneled walls. The marble fireplace was stained black from smoke and filled with the ashes of many fires. Floor-to-ceiling bookshelves contained old books that looked like they'd been thumbed through several times. The parlor had an established, lived-in look, despite the fact that Delia had only recently moved in.

"Hello," I called, and then more loudly, "hello."

No one answered.

I walked through the parlor to the kitchen, which also wasn't occupied. I suddenly envisioned Fat Goldman sitting at the long wooden table, his elbows spread out in front of him, his face pressed against the wood, his enormous ass drooping down over the edges of the cushionless chair. I imagined an empty two-liter container rolling along the floor as his fatness was branded by the hard furniture.

Delia's father had purchased this apartment long after Goldman had left for California; still, I pictured his head lolling on the table.

The gas stove was made of thick iron casting. I opened the squeaky door and discovered more ashes. A black pot had been left on top of the stove. I reached into the pot and touched the cold liquid.

I sat at the table, suppressing an urge to "round" through the apartment.

I was still sitting there several minutes later when a telephone began to ring. I expected to hear Delia's familiar answering machine static, but after two rings, the ringing stopped. Had she answered the phone in one of the bedrooms? The sudden sound and then its cessation made me feel more like a trespasser. I jumped out of the chair and ran to hide in a small room off the kitchen.

This room smelled medicinal, but I couldn't identify anything specific beyond the acrid smells of Lysol and ammonia. The design of the apartment suggested this should be a servant's room, but the fact that it was barren except for a sheetless bed suggested to me that no one was using it. The Meduccis had acquired this apartment after Sal died, nevertheless, I imagined him sweating from fever on the bare bed, reaching to the windowsill for a bowl of cold soup.

The telephone rang, again two rings before stopping. This time I heard the floorboards creak.

Next to the bed, a small window was framed from outside by the branches of an oak tree. I unlocked the window and pulled it up with all my strength, causing a loud screeching sound, a sound that must have been heard throughout the apartment.

Looking out the window, I planned my escape. Still I stayed.

Time was continuing on, past the late afternoon of my arrival at the apartment, and on into the early evening. The sky remained light. It highlighted the bare tree branches as they moved below me in the wind, nets of catch me, gentle swayers of catch me if they had to. But I could see past the tree to a clearing, an opening that had not been made by men under union contract. This was where the water began. The river carried chunks of ice and had the consistency of broken glass as it headed south along the city, then continued beyond it, to the harbor of the sea.

I never heard the door creak. Was it before or after I saw the reflection of his red spectacles in the window glass that I felt the bony hand squeezing a crease into my shoulder? Which perception was the greater horror?

"Breaking and entering," Dr. William Kell said.

He stood beside the bed, posturing pompously, one hand convulsing uncontrollably in the pocket of his Japanese dressing gown. So Kell was the greatest of Delia's trophies. I was surprised that *he* wasn't concerned at being discovered like this; a married man, a prominent member of the faculty, in his nightclothes in a student's apartment in the middle of the day. The professor of medicine reduced to a clown; weakened and controlled by Delia as she first made him feel young and powerful and then took it away.

She was an expert at making a man feel special before rejecting him. In seeing Kell like this, I finally saw how ridiculous I was, we all were—Delia's lovers.

But, Kell still had all the authority. I was a bug to be swatted.

"Where's Delia?" I asked.

"I should call the police."

"The door was open."

"You're lying."

"How do you think I got in?"

Kell paused, considering what I said. If I'd broken in through a locked door, surely he'd have heard the noise.

"It's still breaking and entering. It's a matter for the police."

"Why don't you call them? . . . Afraid of what they'll ask you?"

"David. If you'll agree to psychiatric help, we can avoid the police."

Kell stood between me and the door. The only unblocked exit was the window. For a moment, I considered it.

Kell seemed startled as I headed directly for him. His hands shook as he stepped back out of my way.

I returned to the kitchen. Delia stood at the stove. She was dressed in jeans and a cotton shirt. Her hair was uncombed. She kept her back to me as I approached her.

"Am I a criminal?" I asked, stopping less than a foot away from her.

She didn't answer me, and she didn't turn around. Was she afraid? Her silence increased my longing. The night before, I'd had a dream in which two trains came up alongside each other and ran together over a short distance. Suddenly one of the trains came to a grinding stop and reversed its direction. There was a great whoosh as air was compressed into the small space between the trains. Then they moved rapidly away from each other.

Now Kell was in the kitchen. He didn't move to protect Delia from me. He hesitated, then sat at the table in the same chair where I'd imagined Fat Goldman.

"You're out of control, Levy. Your career is finished."

"I'm not afraid of you, Kell. You're just another professor fucking his student."

"Throw him out of here!" Kell demanded.

But as Delia turned to face us, she began to laugh, a high-pitched hysterical shriek that completely unnerved me. Then she looked at me with a look so intimate that it restored my most irrational hope. It was like the look of a lover awakening from sleep. A forgiving by the body that took absolute precedence. She'd hardly bothered to know me before she'd cast me aside. Was she returning now to her memory of these times?

Months before, Sal and I had arrived at the Bellevue elevator just as the huge steel doors were closing. Delia and Goldman were inside. He was smirking over his conquest. But Delia had been staring at Sal with a look as suggestive as this one. The doors closed. In a fury, with no real hope of catching the pair, Sal ran to the stairs.

What would he have done if he'd caught them? He'd overcome the witch in Catskill with the force of his personality. With Delia though, it was different. Sal was fearful, vulnerable.

"This is ridiculous," Kell said presently, and he pounded the table with his fist.

By any convention, he was right. He was visiting his girlfriend and he was being interrupted by a jealous maniac. But Delia was erratic; perhaps she liked the boldness of my coming here. She had the power to choose, and then, having chosen, to reverse her choice. She could lift the authority from Kell and bestow it on me, arbitrarily.

"Come here," Kell said to her.

But she stayed at the stove with me, now resting her hand on my shoulder. It was absurd, but as long as Delia ordained it, even my breaking into the apartment was a nonevent.

I could see that she was bored with Kell, bored with the control she had over him. My arrival had surprised her—an old lover became her new distraction. She looked at Kell with disgust and seemed ready to betray him. All at once her betrayal took the form I'd long been hoping for.

"You kept hounding Sal," she said to Kell. "You and your fucking study. Anything for another patient. You told him he had to do it to be an intern again. He didn't believe you, but he didn't know how to fight you."

"Where was he?" I asked.

"Hastings. He came back there the day before he died. Bill had the key too, and he went up there without my knowing it. Bill badgered and threatened Sal until Sal left again in his car."

Bill Kell, I thought.

"And that was the end," I said to Kell. "Did you follow him?"

Delia shook her head no, but Kell didn't answer. I didn't think he would ever respond to this question. He hid his face in his hands, slumping forward in Goldman's imagined place.

I left the kitchen and walked toward the front of the apartment. Delia followed me.

"Where do you think you're going?" she demanded.

"I thought I was trespassing."

Kell came running after us, some of his arrogance restored. "You're crazy, Levy," he declared. "Obsessed. And believe me, you're still in plenty of trouble for coming in here like this."

I was becoming more and more tired of them, and sadder as I thought of Sal. To finally see Delia's superficiality was to see a way out that Sal had tragically missed. And Sal could have overcome Kell as well, if only Delia's spell over him had worn off in time.

I finally realized I could just walk away from her, bolstered by the idea that I hardly knew her, that we'd only had sex a few times. My earlier lament, that we'd never established a real relationship, was now my relief. Sadly, I'd allowed her to capitalize on my need for approval.

As I reached the front door of the apartment, Delia tried to prevent me from leaving. She sank her fingernails into my arm and held on to me. At the same time, Kell hugged her, clinging to her like a child. Her breasts heaved as she flung him off. Her physical effort to rid herself of

Kell allowed me to pull myself free, and I was able to get out the door.

The Toyota wouldn't start. As I rolled it down the hill and jumped in, letting out the clutch, I began to laugh uncontrollably. By rejecting Delia, I'd reclaimed my life. I was free.

Angela Santana defended me to The Boss, and after several memos back and forth, she was successful. I did my work. I received reappointment papers for the following year. Angela said that Dr. Kell did not contest my continued employment.

After that, I worked more effectively than ever. I spent my coffee breaks in the library, reading medicine. I stayed late into the night even when I wasn't on call, trying to make up for the last few months. I became known among the other interns as the intern who never wanted to go home. The nurses respected me and didn't try to date me. Several patients asked to be assigned to my care. The residents looked forward to teaching me. By the end of my internship year, I was known throughout Bellevue Hospital as one of the hardest working interns in the program.

PART SIX

THE HOSPITAL OF LAST RESORT

July 1st—The Present

15

*It is July again, and I am finally a resi*dent. I am paid an additional dollar per hour to supervise interns. There is so much medicine I still don't know, but whatever I do know, I try to teach. I pass on the dogma that was passed on to me. A resident must remember what it was like to be an intern. A new resident must not become what he so recently despised.

For my first rotation, I have been given a prestigious assignment. I supervise a group of the best interns and students. They meet with me every morning on the same ward where I met with Goldman last year. My next rotation is due to take place on the wards of

University Hospital. I have gone from outcast to preferred status in just a few months. There hasn't been time for me to acquire the clinical acumen of a Santana or a Goldman, but perhaps my skills are now above average. Most of my newfound popularity is due to Santana. She is the second Bellevue resident in ten years to publish a paper in *The New England Journal of Medicine.* The title is "Unusual Viral Transmission Routes." She has listed me as second author, though my only contribution was to check the references. As a result of this publication, Angela is a shoo-in for chief residency, and I am now popular among my peers.

The interns I supervise are graduates of this medical school, and they know their way around Bellevue. They don't require much assistance, which is fortunate, because I am not always available to assist them. As a resident, I have quickly grown tired of the day-to-day chores of the ward. I despise IVs. I no longer draw blood. I try to find time for a short nap in the on-call rooms before each grueling night as the on-call resident. As a resident, I am expected to write detailed admission notes on every new p atient. I can finally comprehend the irritation Chief Resident Goldman felt when he was stuck with an extra ward tour. When I think of Fat Goldman, I understand more what he was going through and blame him less for Sal's death. At the same time, I have vowed never to ridicule or disempower an intern the way Goldman did. It should be possible to have his authority without causing as much damage. Assigning us the Swan-Ganz catheter to insert into the heart on the first day of internship still seems less like a harmless prank than a nefarious scheme that could have killed a patient.

Nevertheless, Fat Goldman has been mythicized by this year's group of interns. His mannerisms and his unhealthy props have already become Bellevue lore. More than half the current interns say they will transfer to a California program unless things at Bellevue improve. One of my new interns, Dr. Appel, was a medical student here under Goldman. Appel has named me "Little Goldman," a designation that is meant as the highest compliment, though I respond with anger whenever I hear it.

Tonight, *my* interns don't know where *I* am. I hide from their constant questions on the balcony of my former patient Victor Rulo, who has finally been granted a room at Bellevue. For the past several weeks he has been a patient on the rehab service. Tonight, while he sleeps, I stand out on his balcony.

The coffee truck arrives at Bellevue and parks in the alcove five floors below me. Interns begin to emerge from the hospital and collect outside by the truck. Traditionally, male interns stand there in the dark and discuss the nurses, planning ahead for moments of freedom. Tonight, the truck is illuminated brightly by an uncovered lamp. My intern Dr. Appel joins the line and waits patiently. He wears thick eyeglasses. He's unshaven; his clothes are crumpled; his back is stooped. I wonder if he takes his cues from my dress, from my low-to-the-ground posture and my thick eyeglasses. Does he discuss the Levy walk with the other interns—the way I project my chin and knees forward, swinging my arms with every step?

As midnight approaches, I "supervise" Appel from above without his knowing it. As he waits on line, a man, one of *the bedless,* approaches him. "I'm dying, but I'm trying," *the bedless* shouts, and Appel hands him some coins. A hundred years ago this "patient" might have received his care on a river quarantine boat. Tonight, he begs change from my intern and then asks for scraps of food from the owner of the coffee truck. Appel looks bewildered. I wonder if he knows he can page me with a problem. I am easily distracted, always preoccupied, but I'm available for my interns if a sudden crisis arises.

I call out to Appel but he doesn't seem to hear me. I'm about to call again when there is a noise behind me. Victor Rulo is coming out to his balcony.

Rulo still intrigues me. "Continuity of care" has failed to bind me to any of my other former patients the way I am bound to Rulo. As a resident, I am quick to forget them all. Inching up the totem pole of authority, I am obsessed only with the importance of having my own interns to command. But I can't seem to forget Rulo. What many consider his craziness, I have taken for wisdom. Despite his delusions, his knowledge is vast. He has predicted future events. Sometimes he seems to be the only sane man at Bellevue. When I was his intern, I ignored sicker patients to answer his complaints. Now that he is no longer assigned to me, I still can't resist a visit. His boldness reminds me of Sal, who shared his disdain for unthinking authority. Unlike them, I find myself obeying.

As Rulo approaches, his smell overwhelms me and I

back away from him, all the way to the rusty railing that defines the edge of the balcony. Many of the old bolts are loose or have fallen off. The railing sways as I lean against it.

I look out to the highway, and the broken guardrail, rebroken from a recent accident, reminds me: The Alfa was returning to Bellevue from the country. Sal had lost all control. At the time, as an intern, I was seeking direction. My resident was unavailable, as I am now temporarily unavailable to my interns. I had only my fledgling training, urging me on to the next dying patient, keeping me (cruelly, I thought) from my time even to grieve. For weeks afterward, the staff gossiped over coffee, while I, member of a group suddenly lacking a member, worked on. Maybe it was the work that kept me going, though when Sal died, it was as if my sickest patients no longer had a chance for lasting cures.

Out on the highway, the traffic is now just a trickle of cars. The longer I stay out here, the less I feel able to leave. I am caught in the memory of the accident and its victim. I miss him so terribly. My doctor's armor doesn't protect me from my anguish. When Rulo sees me start to cry, he doesn't leave me alone. He doesn't roll back inside to the small comfort of his hard Bellevue bed. I can feel his anger welling up too; he seems to remember what I remember.

I wipe my face and watch my intern down there, as optimistic as I was at the beginning, yet about to be overwhelmed by the patients' pain and the staff's indifference. It is my role to reach out to him, to nurture him and guide him through. But I am barely out of internship myself. My new identity is a gloss over the great pain I suffered as an intern.

I recover myself and call again to him. But at the same moment another *bedless* man approaches him, shouting in his face. Appel probably doesn't hear me over the noise of *the bedless*. Staring at him, Appel reaches nervously into his pocket and brings out more change.

Rulo has been rolling closer to me, bit by bit, until there is now no escaping him. I am pinned between his wheelchair and the railing. When he is right on top of me, Rulo no longer seems to be a genius. I wonder; how can I have accepted his view of Bellevue?

He laughs, displaying his broken teeth. His wheelchair rolls an inch backward, and I am able to slip by him.

"Take me to the University," he insists, rolling after me. "Do something to get me there."

"But, Victor. You hate University Hospital."

"Who is left to help me here? You?"

"Not me. I'm no longer your intern."

"Must I wait until a ferry comes?"

"Where are you going to sleep tonight if University refuses you?"

"Sleep?" Rulo says. "How can you speak of sleep? I was in five Stalinist prisons after the war. Do you think I slept?"

"But you finally have a room here. You have a bed. A tranquil view."

"Bellevue is a boneyard, the end of the line for doctors and patients. Over at the University, every toilet has a carpeted seat, every wall has a commissioned painting, every hall, a statue or a sculpture. Doctors exhibit their tie collections. They bill their patients for a five-minute visit. The wards are named for billionaire benefactors. Bellevue is the hospital of last resort. Before, no other hospital would take me. Now I can go anywhere. I am a curiosity. I have completed a clinical trial. I am a medical success."

"You said you were mistreated at University Hospital. Now you want to go back?"

"I've reconsidered. At the University, one nurse is assigned to every three patients. A patient in good standing is permitted to eat in the gourmet cafeteria."

"A patient in good standing?"

"Over at the University, patients are now treated with traditional medications. They no longer participate in barbaric protocols."

Apparently, Dr. Kell's power at University Hospital has been diminished by more senior members of the faculty. The Bellevue study still pays for his wardrobe, his bright red sedan, his tropical time-share. But at University Hospital, Dr. Kell has been reduced to just five hours per week in the faculty office suite.

Santana has protested against Kell's study in memo after memo. She believes the study involves injecting a patient with dead *virus* in search of a vaccine. The potential for profit and glory is enormous. But is *the virus* administered to patients really dead? The research and development committee at University Hospital has finally blocked the study. Bellevue, on the other hand, with Kell as a member of the research and development committee, has less regard for patient safety. Perhaps Kell believes it would be impossible to blame the study for transmitting *the virus* in a hospital where biters roam the halls.

Santana has been unable to verify her suspicion. The Boss and his lieutenants have flatly denied her allegation, responding to each of her memos with a memo of their own. Despite the pressure Santana has put on them, they have continued to treat her well, which adds to my belief that Kell has lost power. Santana intends to have the red liquid analyzed under the electron microscope for proof, but recently all study bags have disappeared from the Bellevue wards.

"Victor, have you been affected by the red liquid?"

Rulo ignores the question. "Take me to the University," he urges.

"But it's almost midnight."

"The last ferry leaves at fifteen past."

"I can't leave my interns and go on a reckless boat ride across the river in the middle of the night."

"I must go tonight," Rulo says simply. "Otherwise I'll die."

"The clerks will never let us in."

Rulo has inched close to me again. He speaks in a conspiratorial whisper. I realize that I am about to hear the truth of why he thinks he needs to go.

"I am a landmark case. If I remain at Bellevue, Dr. Kell plans to restudy me. If I survive it, the results will be used to attract more volunteers. If I refuse, he still can study me if I ever fall asleep."

Rulo is my friend. Even if he is exaggerating, I know I will take him across the river to improve his care, to remove him once and for all from the clutches of Kell. At University Hospital, perhaps Rulo will finally accept a social worker's plan for his discharge.

If only I'd been able to do the same for Sal. Would Sal have lived if he'd been admitted to University Hospital instead of Bellevue?

"In Dr. Vertino's memory," Rulo says, seeming to intuit my thoughts.

Five floors below us, Appel is looking around with a Where's Levy? expression on his face. Nevertheless, I turn away and wheel Rulo from the balcony. We pass through his room and out into the hall. No one stops me as I wheel him to the elevators. An elevator is waiting with its doors open. It is full of refuse, empty of passengers. This year the state legislature has proposed across-the-board cuts in funding to all the public hospitals. The number of ambulances will be reduced by half. Ferry service across the river will be suspended. In anticipation of these proposed changes, the number of patient admissions to Bellevue has already been reduced substantially, and the elevators are often empty.

We reach the ground floor. I push Rulo through the ER, his Hades. Tonight there are only three occupied stretchers against the alcove walls, and the smell here is surprisingly medicinal—and stronger than Rulo's unwashed smell. As we reach the emergency entrance, Rulo's wheels touch the mat. For once the glass doors slide open without delay. It is very hot outside, almost ninety degrees. My intern Appel is now no longer on line at the coffee truck.

Rulo's eyes are closed as I take him toward the river. The unexpected heat outside staggers me, slowing my pace. Finally, I reach the concrete underbelly of the highway. Cars roar over my head. As I move Rulo in between the stanchions, wafts of cooler air come up off the river and soothe me, drying my sweat.

Five *bedless* stretchers remain under the highway. *The bedless* wave at us as I bring Rulo to the tree by the edge of the concrete. In May, an unidentified patient wielding an ax hacked up this tree. By July, it still hasn't produced a single bloom.

A large boat is positioned sideways at the shore, moored to three floating logs. The sign on the side of the boat reads UNIVERSITY SHUTTLE.

I roll Rulo up the ramp and onto the boat. He insists that I take him to the front deck. We pass through the inside cabin. A disheveled man sits amid rows of empty seats. His hair is clumped, and his skin is scaly red, as if he has been scalded by a total-body burn.

"It's *the virus,*" Rulo whispers.

The man stares at the floor as we pass him.

Two nurses from the Bellevue emergency room smoke cigarettes and gossip to each other in the front row of the cabin. They glance at Rulo.

"It's the living textbook," one of them says.

"Dr. Levy," the other says. "Aren't you supposed to be at Bellevue?"

I don't answer. In truth, I still haven't signed out for the night to the covering resident. Am I AWOL in the Goldman tradition? My interns can still page me, can reach me on the other side of the river. But if there is a code, I won't be able to help, and the covering resident will have to take over. This is the first group of interns I've ever commanded. When they stay until midnight to complete their work, I feel I should be available as well. Yet I also feel justified participating in Rulo's elopement. It is a worthwhile adventure, in memory of an adventurer.

Rulo and I reach the front deck as a foghorn blows and the deckhands release the boat from the makeshift dock.

Once we're under way, the salt spray on my face refreshes me, and it revives Rulo. The midnight ferry chugs ahead through the dark water, passing a small buoy. A fluorescent arrow points east toward University Hospital. Rulo is quiet as he gazes overboard. The water sprays up over the deck and paints our faces with salt.

I haven't seen Delia since abandoning her apartment. Angela told me that Delia has arranged to take all her fourth-year-student electives in Europe.

"Does this bother you?" Angela asked me.

"No," I replied. "I don't care what she does."

Angela smiled.

But I continue to actively despise Kell. I avoid all conferences and grand rounds that he might attend.

Our interns may not know it yet, but Fat Goldman is no longer in California. In June, I received a postcard with the news that he was vacating his plush post and accepting a research position in Tennessee, his home state. Several of our residents say they've left messages for him on his new answering machine there, but he hasn't called them back.

Sally Wilson is applying for admission to medical school. I speak with her twice a month by telephone. We have arranged to meet for coffee several times, but one of us has always canceled. I frequently imagine getting back together with Sally, though I never do.

Last week I telephoned Giuseppe Vertino.

"Don't be calling here looking for my sympathy," he said.

"I called to see how *you* were."

"You mustn't give in. Continue on with your work. Be the best doctor you can be. How am I? You want to know how I am? I lie in my bed all night without sleeping. When the wind comes up, I hear rustling sounds. I wonder if someone could be out there in the woods."

Giuseppe seemed inconsolably sad. A father who'd lost a son and then a grandson, he repeated lessons I was learning on my own.

"Did the hospital ever contact you?" I asked him.

"They wanted authorization for a plaque. I refused. Someone asked a lot of foolish questions about Sal's childhood."

"Dr. Bruner?"

"No. Bruner never had the decency to call me. This was one of his assistants."

"Anyone else?"

"That woman of Sal's—said she wanted to come here and talk with me. Like a fool I agreed, but then she never came."

As I gaze east from the front deck of the boat, the river seems narrow, as if a few thrusts of the engine will be enough to bring us to the shore. But the boat chugs slowly along, chopping through the river bilge. I see the occasional condom swirling in the surf. Rulo calls it a whitefish.

University Hospital looms before us. The glass walls reflect back the lights of our approaching boat. As it reaches the shore, the ferry turns and maneuvers in sideways against a large metallic dock.

The deckhands loop the cables over the mooring posts as the off-duty nurses clatter down the ramp. They ignore the struggles of the red-skinned patient as he clings to the railing. As I pass, he grabs my shoulder, and I help him down the ramp, wheeling Rulo down at the same time.

Rulo and I head for the main entrance to University Hospital. The clerk stops us just before the large glass doors.

"Pawns controlling us!" Rulo shouts.

"Let him go!" I order the clerk. "On my authority. Let him pass!" I wave my arms in the air and the clerk hesitates, but then he seems to recognize me and nods that Rulo can enter. Now Rulo is grinning. He rises up out of his wheelchair, and I remember my dream, where he was the jogger. Perhaps Sally Wilson was right—Rulo could walk all along.

He leans on his eight-ball walking stick for two hobbled, faltering steps. "Faker!" I yell, and he smiles and casts his support away altogether. The black stick goes skittering along the flawless pavement, as Rulo walks straight to the entrance of University Hospital and passes beyond its doors.

"Good-bye, Dr. Levy." His voice trails off as he disappears inside.

"See you next month," I call after him.

I will be a resident at University next month. This month, I am still supposed to be at Bellevue. Now that Rulo is gone, I feel guilty for abandoning my interns. Turning back to the river, I see that the deckhands have shut off the boat's electricity, closing it down for the night. The BELLEVUE SHUTTLE sign on *this* side of the boat is dark.

How I am going to get back? Across the river, I can barely see Bellevue. As a result of growing austerity measures, there are only a few emergency lights, blinking on and off at irregular intervals. "They haven't paid their electric bill," I say aloud, though no one seems to hear me.

I head toward the parking lot in the hope that I can find someone to drive me back across the river. I walk along a road with sparkling pavement, ascending the same tree-lined hill down which Sally Wilson and I once push-started the Toyota. I feel very lonely. I know I am hoping that by some wonderful coincidence Sally herself will be coming off her shift at University Hospital, and we will meet for the first time in months at the entrance to the Meducci garden, funds for which were donated by Delia's father.

But the garden is deserted. I discover to my horror the Salvatore Vertino memorial plaque with its spotlighted inscription: THE PATIENTS ARE THE TEACHERS. Despite Giuseppe's refusal, the plaque has been placed here. It is bronze; it has a marble base. It is flanked by a park bench and a bubbling water fountain on one side, and on the other side, rows and rows of flowers.

I grieve because Sal is only in the past. As my facility as a physician grows, I will move further from the memory, until one day even Bellevue will become part of my past. The garden, these streets, the glass buildings all seem more familiar to me than I can justify. Perhaps I will attain the rank of University faculty. Rulo has predicted it. The University is in my future.

I find my way from the garden to the parking lot. I arrive at the emergency entrance just as an ambulance is pulling in. Paramedics of the graveyard shift remove a stretcher. They snap it open, ready to roll. They bring a patient out. He has curly hair and resembles Larcombe. The paramedics transfer the patient onto the stretcher and begin to pump on his chest right there in the parking lot.

"Let me help," I say as I approach, and one of the paramedics responds to my confidence by saying, "Take over."

The ambulance has all the medications I need, and between me and the two paramedics, we run a tight little code on the patient, who begins to recover. My sense of purpose envelops me. I am a physician in training. My skills are becoming more usable by the day.

One of the paramedics smiles and says, "This one is going to make it."

When I arrive at Bellevue the following morning at 8:15, Appel is already at the chart rack, but my other intern hasn't yet come. My medical students are also waiting; I'm embarrassed that I can't remember their names. These two are similar to Michael and Bruce: studious, eager to please, eager to join me in not respecting Appel. In fact, I'm annoyed when he doesn't know the latest lab results or when he's forgotten to check on a patient's chest X ray. Why don't I apply the same standards to my other intern? He never comes to rounds on time. He's always flirting with the nurses. He's much more likely to kill a patient, but I'm afraid of him decompensating from my criticism.

Why have I been assigned only two medical students instead of three? Would the third one have been a woman? Would I have pursued her?

As I come down the hall toward the chart rack, Appel is watching me all the way. I'm still wearing yesterday's clothes, crumpled from having slept in them. In fact, I slept alongside the dock, taking the first ferry back across the river at 7 A.M.

I reach the chart rack and remove the chart of Appel's most difficult patient.

"How's the living lab test?" I say.

Appel doesn't respond right away.

"Where were you last night?" he says, glaring. "We needed you here."

I say nothing, an old Goldman trick. The longer I make Appel wait, the more my authority is reestablished.

But we don't wait very long, because the cardiac arrest beeper goes off, disrupting rounds before they've even started. Most days, we don't make it through rounds. Sick patients call us away. I'm comfortable with this, even if my interns—starved for teaching—aren't.

I run along the hall, heading for the code, ready to take charge. Appel and the two students follow along behind. They stay close to me. I am all they have. They remind me of imprinting ducklings.

Halfway to the code, my other intern joins the group. He is tall, muscular, unshaven, wearing surgical scrubs instead of the intern's white uniform. I imagine that he's been out all night with one of the nurses. When he sees me looking at him, he immediately calls out, "Slow down, Levy. Where the hell are you going so fast?" as if a patient's dying will wait for us to arrive. And then off to the side I hear Appel. Directing his words to the medical students, Appel grumbles, "Little Goldman sure runs a lot faster than Fat Goldman did."